The Styx Trilogy
Book Three

Recast Light

by
Rose Corcoran

To
the "Me"
from eleven years ago,
for starting this great adventure
and for never giving up

♠♦♣♥♣♦♠

Table of Contents

Prologue

Several Minutes Before Dawn

The clock overlooking the rooftop terrace struck fourteen, and the goblin in the long, embroidered coat paced impatiently. Sebastian knew from experience that Chiaroscuran clocks had nothing to do with day or night, concepts which were merely academic or aesthetic to most of the city's inhabitants, but that it must be almost sunrise by now.

Looking up past the Empyreal Palace's white walls, he saw only blackness above, as usual. Alcea had assured him it would happen soon, that this city would be drawn out of the crumbling shadow that surrounded it into the safety of daylight, but so far, nothing had changed. He had stayed up all night watching the sky and once again felt fatigued, but refused to rest— still unused to sleep and suspicious of it. Hopefully, he thought, his recent repose—which had allowed Millicent and Misha to escape—had been some sort of anomaly. Additionally, he wanted to savor his last free moments.

"This city really is something," a sultry voice said. He turned to see a goat-like goblin walking toward him.

"Shouldn't you be in disguise?"

She changed into a tall human with black hair and glasses, saying, "I doubt anyone will see us. And I really don't care if they do. Soon everything will be just the way I want it."

Sebastian couldn't help but smile down on the rows of black and white rooftops surrounding the palace, thinking of all his people who had never seen the sun. Alcea huffed and sat on the rail in her shadow goblin form in a vain attempt to block the city from his view.

"You're far too attached to these mortal creatures for your own good," she said. "It really isn't healthy."

"I don't think you're one to lecture me about unhealthy attachments. I've seen the collection in your cave."

"Those are my treasured possessions. Each of them will last nearly as long as I will. Surely you don't think art like this is worthless?" She waved a hand toward the statues and carvings of the palace.

"Of course not, but the people who made it are more important. Even the most beautiful city is nothing without its people."

Alcea turned away from him without a word, giving him an unpleasant feeling. He couldn't dwell on this, however, for he was blinded by a flash of light as the stone floor beneath them shuddered. An instant later, Sebastian felt something cold and wet coming down on him. When his vision returned, he looked up to see dark gray clouds sending a torrent of rain over the city.

"Where are we?" he asked, staring to the edge of the city where wet blades of grass blew in the wind, making the hills they covered look like green ocean waves.

"We're in the Wastes." Alcea said, having turned into a

leather-clad Gremlin. "You can still see several trash piles over that way. The mapmaker must have changed some things. I imagine she redrew that hideous mound that cast the shadow as the city itself."

Sebastian had a tinge of guilt for causing the destruction of Heather's last map and extreme gratitude for the improved landscape surrounding the city.

"Now onto more important matters," Alcea continued, pulling the contract out of her coat. The paper did not appear to soak in any moisture, and the ink did not run, but rather, had begun to glow. She held the contract up and instructed Sebastian to touch it. As soon as he placed his fingers on his signature, he felt a strange sting. It was not exactly painful, but was certainly unpleasant, and as it began to creep up his arm, the words on the contract moved towards his fingers, slowly disappearing as if he were siphoning them into his own body. The stinging sensation lessened, eventually disappearing altogether. Alcea looked at the blank piece of paper, which hung limply in her hands as the rain soaked it, then tossed it away.

"Shall we go to your cave, then?" Sebastian asked, glancing up at the palace for what he was sure would be his last time.

"We'll be staying here for a while longer." She headed toward the doors to the palace, a shadow goblin once again. "I want to check the buildings' foundations, in case that rumbling damaged anything. One broken pillar could bring this whole city crashing down. As for you, make sure the Chiaroscurans stay within the city limits. I can't protect them if they leave.

She sounded sincere, but Sebastian knew she was only thinking of the terms of their contract. He was only bound to serve her if she kept the city safe.

"Alcea…"

"Call me Hollyhock."

"Hollyhock," he found himself saying, "if we're no longer in a shadow, that means Delilah has found out about us."

"And?"

"As far as I'm concerned, any contact she has with this city will be detrimental."

"I'll protect it," Alcea said with a sneer. "Even from her."

One

Let Sleeping Dogsbodies Lie

Hello, Hello, Bostwick! How are you? I am fine. Isn't that a weird way to start a letter?

Bostwick blinked, adjusted the hat in his hands, and reread the writing on a small purple note he had found on the floor outside his bedroom.

Anyway, I was going to wake you up with everyone else, but Emmaline assured me it would be like waking a belligerent wyrm (or something like that!), so I decided to play it safe and tell you the good news via note. I got Chiaroscuro out of the shadow! Actually, Heather did, but that's beside the point. To celebrate, we were going to have a picnic, but it's raining, so we'll just eat inside.

Now stop lollygagging and go to the ballroom to help Millie with brunch!

Love and Chaos,

Delilah

"Brunch?" he mumbled, noticing a small downward-pointing arrow drawn at the bottom of the page. He turned it over and read, *Brunch: A goblinical concept that describes the meal half-way between breakfast and—*

"I know what brunch is!" he said, walking up the hall.

"How does she manage to be so annoying when she isn't even here?"

When he got to the ballroom, he saw Emmaline and Millicent already setting the table. the former busily arranging knives, forks, and napkins while the latter carried stacks of pancakes from a platter to each plate.

"Good morning, Bostwick!" Millicent said.

"I thought Delilah went to get you up half an hour ago," said Emmaline. "What happened?"

He handed her Delilah's note rather than explain, and asked, "So is Chiaroscuro really safe?"

"It is!" Millicent said. "Delilah showed me with a telescope this morning. It's sitting in the Wastes right where that garbage pile used to be. She already sent Misha to tell their Council that they're all official citizens of Styx!"

"Where is she, anyway?"

"Talking with the Roly Police to make sure the town made it back safely," Emmaline said, "and to be sure all the citizens and shops are accounted for. That much can't be said for the castle." She indicated the dingy cutlery and chipped dishes laid out on the table. "It looks like someone made off with the silverware and fine china, and I noticed some dirty scuff marks outside the treasure chamber door when I passed."

"It was probably some Catawampian. I wouldn't put it past them."

"Still, everything else seems to be all right," Millicent said and began to count the pancakes on each plate, humming to herself as she did so.

Bostwick was relieved to see her in better spirits than last night, when it seemed that the entire fate of Chiaroscuro had rested on her shoulders. With that out of the way, the only thing left to deal with was Sebastian and his death wish, which, considering his immortality, was not nearly as urgent. Things could start going back to normal like she wanted and then, maybe once everything had settled down, and the time was right, he could tell her…

Millicent noticed him watching her and smiled back, before tilting her head curiously at the object in his hands.

"Is that my hat, Bostwick?" she asked, pointing to the small yellow and green top hat.

"Before," Bostwick said, coming back to reality, "when I thought we had to escape from Delilah, I assumed you would want it with you. The rest of your things are still in the airship. Delilah gave it to you, didn't she?"

Millicent nodded, taking the hat. "She bought it for me when she first agreed to teach me magic. She said any student of hers would have to be well dressed, so we went to a hat shop the very first day we met. The milliner in the Capital tried to talk me into getting a darker color, since magicians are supposed to be more formal, but Delilah threatened to… Well, never mind." She turned the hat around in her hands a few times, then placed it on her head and straightened it with a levitation spell. "Of course, it ought to be pinned on. And I really shouldn't be wearing it until after graduation, but, well, you know…"

"Speaking of which," Emmaline said. "Now that we know the truth about the admittance test, why *don't* we tell the Academy about it?"

"What do you mean?"

"Well, aside from the fact that the current administration should be informed about the goblin experimentation that happened at their school, there's the fact that you only failed the test because you studied Alistair's notes. If they let you take it again, I'm sure you could pass it."

"You mean… go to the Academy? Me?"

"The place could use more students like you, honestly," Bostwick said, then noticed her nervously knitting her fingers together. "What's wrong?"

"N-nothing."

It was an obvious lie, as Millicent had wanted to attend that school since she was a child. Bostwick thought she would've jumped at the chance.

"Is it… because of what Sebastian showed you?"

"It's not that." She glanced up at Bostwick, bit her lip like she was thinking of saying something, then quickly looked away. "I-I mean, of course I *want* to go. I'm just not sure… you know… that they'll let me. That's all."

"Well—" Emmaline began, but was interrupted by Clarence's voice, booming through the hall outside. "So they're finally coming." She sighed, walking to the door. "Delilah probably neglected to wake them up as well."

Bostwick turned back to Millicent, catching her hat for her as the levitation spell ended.

"Thanks," she said, still sounding nervous. He handed the hat back to her and she stared into it, blushing slightly, but not meeting his eye.

Maybe things wouldn't go back to normal after all.

♠ ♦ ♣ ♥ ♣ ♦ ♠

After brunch, they decided to go around the castle to see if anything else was amiss after its return from Catawampus. While Clarence offered to explore the lower floors and Dolly claimed the library, Emmaline wisely suggested that the throne room would be a good place to start.

"What happened to the clock!" Millicent cried.

Pieces of green and yellow glass lay scattered across the floor where they had fallen after the castle's abrupt arrival in Catawampus. Rainwater had pooled around and under these, and continued to pour in through the clock's exposed gears. The throne had been thoroughly drenched.

"Let's just say we had a bumpy landing when the castle moved," Emmaline said. "I didn't think about the rain, though. What should we do?"

"We have to clean up the water! Oh, but I don't want anyone to get cut… um, and maybe we could use a tarp for that window?"

"We can probably fix it using magic," Bostwick said. "Though I'm not sure where all the pieces go. When Delilah gets back, she can hopefully tell us—"

"*Bostwick!*" Delilah cried, marching into the room as if on cue. "What *have* you done to my throne room?" Bostwick grimaced, not dignifying her with a response, so she flung her soaking coat at him and held her hands up to frame the shattered window. "I suppose I can supervise. Millie, why don't you focus on those bigger pieces. Bostwick, you handle the little shards. Just pretend you're fixing a watch face."

"How did things go in town?" Millicent asked, carefully joining two pieces of a large yellow pane together. The crack between them disappeared as she cast her spell.

"All citizens are accounted for and most of the buildings seem to be holding up. Of course, Styx owes Polkory an enormous amount of money for all her items given to that immortal beast. The police said everything's gone swimmingly, though they weren't exactly helpful."

"With what?"

"Hmm? Oh, Bostwick, that piece you just fixed goes with that dodo-shaped bit."

"Right," he said, "but what did you need the police's help with?"

"Oh, nothing, really…"

"Nothing?"

"Why, Emmaline," she said, ignoring his question, "you're staring off into space. How uncharacteristically Bostwickian of you. Is something wrong?"

"What? Oh… not exactly," Emmaline said. "After all, Styx is back together, Millicent's all right, and you've made sure Chiaroscuro is safe, which means I should be going back to Camellia soon. I am homesick, and I really want to see my family, but I'm going to miss everyone here."

"You can come visit us," Millicent said.

"Maybe… I don't know how much free time I'll have. Even though I'm the youngest and don't have a lot to do, I've neglected my duties for over a year now."

"Being cursed doesn't exactly count as 'neglecting one's duties'," Bostwick said, repairing his tenth window pane. "Though I'm sure your family probably wants you to stay home for a while. And you'll have to make sure the new court magician does his job right."

"New magician?" Millicent asked.

"Mr. Charles was looking for one when we went to the Academy. I'm still supposed to work here for eighty years." He shot Delilah an accusing glance. "Though I could just leave, considering you can't actually curse me."

"Don't be absurd," Delilah said. "I'm sure Camellia already has more butlers than they know what to do with. Another one would just get underfoot. The same goes for princesses, too, I'm sure."

"I suppose they'll be all right without me," Emmaline said, "and Mr. Charles did say that my duty right now is to the people of Styx. I just can't help wondering how much help I'll be, now that everything seems to be taking care of itself."

"Well, you know what they say: Noblesse, No-blige."

"Nobody says that."

"Hmm, well. As long as you're here, I might need your help dealing with some of the more sticky situations in Chiaroscuro."

"Meaning what?" Bostwick asked.

"Nothing in particular." She waved her hand airily, then snatched up Bostwick's hat. "Anyway, I'll be borrowing this for a bit. No worries; you'll get it back this afternoon. Just keep fixing that glass and let me deal with the internal affairs of state."

With that, she left through one of the secret passages.

"Millicent, will you be all right fixing the rest of these?" Bostwick asked, placing a newly fixed piece of glass on the floor. "Something about what she said seems awfully suspicious."

He went through the door Delilah had taken and found a

narrow spiral staircase that led up to the treasure chamber. Delilah was examining a case of various weapons when she noticed that she had been followed.

"Leaving Millie to fix everything by herself, eh, Bostwick? That's another fifty years to your sentence."

"What?"

"Just kidding. I assume you have something interesting to tell me. It's about your talk with Millie last night, isn't it?"

"No."

"Then Emmaline. Is it about Emmaline?"

"Stop changing the subject. What's going on with the Chiaroscuro? There's something you're not telling us."

"Oh, Bostwick, I would never hide something from you—"

"Unless it was for comedic effect. Yes. I've heard that before. What happened last time was so hilarious, after all."

Delilah pouted her lips, then grabbed his shoulder and led him over to a large musical instrument that sat in the corner of the room farthest from the door. She glanced around conspiratorially before speaking.

"All right. I'll tell you, but you must be sworn to secrecy." She took a deep breath, then said, "Misha sold me his memories to warn me that Alcea is going to try and blow up Chiaroscuro with a devastating Gremlin bomb."

"What!"

"Shush. He almost failed abysmally, of course. It's a good thing Millie brought him here, or I might not have used his memories until it was far too late. He left last night to try and warn Sebastian about the whole affair."

"But why does Alcea want to kill her own people?"

"Who knows? The point is, she has to be stopped, and I'm the only one for the job."

"But you just said that Sebastian's going to find out about it. If he isn't bound to serve Alcea…"

"You have a point, but no. No, Sebastian is far too incompetent. He failed to make Millie kill him; he failed to destroy Styx; I'm sure if we left him with this task he'd only end up blowing himself up. Hmm, on purpose, perhaps. Anyway, I'm sure he'd just fail, as usual, so I have to do this myself."

"And you aren't telling anyone because…?"

"If I told them, they'd tell Millie, of course." Delilah tugged on her hair and sighed. "She's so happy, Bostwick. Right now, she just needs to focus on being back home. I don't want to upset her since everything finally seems to be going so well."

"Because trying to keep things from Millicent in order to spare her feelings has never blown up in your face before."

"You were the one doing the blowing up that time, Mr. I'll-side-with-a-cat-instead-of-my-dear-employer. But that's in the past. I trust you to keep this a secret."

"I still think we should tell her."

"Hmm? You really want to ruin her day?"

"I'll tell her tonight, then," he said sarcastically.

"And ruin dinner?"

"I'll tell her *after* dinner, okay? Don't you think, after everything she went through with Sebastian, she deserves to be told exactly what's going on for once?"

"Is that so? Then why don't you tell her how you feel about her? Doesn't she deserve to know that?"

"Actually," Bostwick said, double checking that that they were alone, "I *was* planning to—"

Delilah made a noise half-way between a scream and a squeal and made to run toward the door before Bostwick jumped in front of her.

"Out of the way!" she cried. "We must tell Millie at once!"

"'We' nothing! *I'm* going to tell her… or, well…"

"Hmmmmm?" she purred.

"I was going to…"

"You coward! This is no time to lose your nerve!"

"It's not like that. I want to tell her, but… Look, Emmaline was thinking, with everything we know about the Academy, and the truth behind their admittance test, there's no reason why Millicent shouldn't be allowed to go there."

"I suppose not," Delilah said, stepping back and narrowing her eyes. "What your point?"

"My point is, Millicent's wanted to go to the Academy her whole life, and I don't want to get in the way of that."

She tapped her gloved index fingers together for a moment, thinking, then said, "Don't be absurd, Bostwick. Millie can continue learning magic from you. She loves you, you silly dodo."

"That's the problem," he said miserably. "I don't want her feelings for me to make her doubt her decision to go to the Academy, and since I'm stuck here—"

"Hmm?"

"I mean, not technically. I know you can't curse me, but…" He fidgeted with his bow tie for a moment, hating Delilah's increasingly gratified grin.

"Why, Bostwick!" she gasped, theatrically throwing her hands over her mouth. "Are you admitting that you feel indebted to me for your previous transgression of stealing my Domino—twice—and that it is your honor, rather than a threat of force that is keeping you bound to me?"

Bostwick did not respond, save for a drawn-out groan.

"*Bostwick!* You're not a scoundrel after all. Well, then, I suppose there is nothing preventing me from giving you my blessing. You may freely seek Millie's hand."

"Her… wh-what? Have you been listening to a single word I've been saying?"

"Oh, that nonsense about Millie leaving us? Or the fact that you're utterly smitten with her but too cold-footed to say anything? Honestly, Bostwick, if you were just going to talk in circles then I don't know why you brought it up."

"You brought it up—"

"Did I?"

"—to distract from the bomb."

"Blast! You remembered."

"Getting back to the matter at hand, I assume you already talked to the police about it, right?"

"They could offer no helpful expertise with a bomb of this variety."

"Then let's see if we can all come up with something to do about it, together. I'm telling everyone about it after dinner. Just try and stop me," he said, and left the room.

"Well, if you make it a challenge," she said with a shrug.

♠ ♦ ♣ ♥ ♣ ♦ ♠

After fixing the throne room window (with some levitational assistance from Clarence) Bostwick, Millicent, and Emmaline spent the afternoon in the library. Millicent performed the tricks she had been practicing during her time in Chiaroscuro while Bostwick corrected her mistakes. She made little progress, as she was preoccupied with Sebastian's request to be annihilated through magic. Emmaline and Bostwick discussed ways to dissuade him from his desire to end his existence, but nothing either of them said seemed particularly convincing. Dolly, who sat in one corner of the library poring over books on herbal medicine, offered to write a list of things that would make life worth living, but Millicent said she was fairly sure that wouldn't work.

After a dinner filled with similar conversation, Millicent still had no idea what to do for Sebastian, but decided that she couldn't give up, no matter what. Everyone else had unanimously decided to go to bed early, with Bostwick looking particularly exhausted, so Millicent went around the castle opening windows to let the cool air in for the night. She was making her way down the card hallway when she caught movement with the corner of her eye.

"Hello?" she said, but received no response. Making her small flame spell as large as possible, she walked to the bend in the hallway, but stopped when she noticed something on the ground. A lasso of rope circled her feet, then went up the wall to where it was rigged through a system of pulleys along the ceiling, then down to where it was being tugged on by a short gray goblin with a leather jacket, two small wings, and an inordinately large mouth. Millicent stepped lightly out of the circle, for the rope had not moved an inch

"Um, hello," she said, causing the goblin to jump.

"Eh, what the—?" he said in a squeaky, scratchy voice. He looked at the rope in his hands, then tried to hide it behind his back as if it weren't there.

"Is this supposed to be one of those traps?" Millicent continued. "Like the one you catch rabbits in? I think your rope is jammed in one of the pulleys."

"Eh, right. Yes. Catching rabbits. That's what I was doing."

Millicent studied him for a moment, then clapped her hands together.

"Oh! You must be from Catawampus and got lost in the castle, right?"

"Exactly!" He offered her a hand that looked like a pig's. "I'm from Catawampus and I got lost. That's what happened."

"Oh, dear. Well, we're in Styx now. The castle moved. Um, it's kind of hard to explain. I'm really sorry about this. My name's Millicent by the way."

"Balder Da—ah, er… Dot," he said, sounding sickened with himself. "Balder Dot. I'm just a regular run-of-the-mill Gremlin who got lost."

"Dot? How cute!" She smiled, oblivious to the Gremlin's scowl. "Well, you can spend the night in one of our guest rooms, and tomorrow Delilah can think of a way to get you back home."

"Much obliged," he said, and followed her up to his new room. "I, um, noticed that device out in the garden. It wouldn't happen to be a flying machine, would it?"

"It's an airship."

"I see. You wouldn't happen to know how to pilot such a thing, now would you?"

"I don't, but Emmaline does. That might not be a bad way to get to Catawampus, actually."

He scrunched his mouth thoughtfully.

"Well, here you are." Millicent stopped before the room that had belonged to Emmaline when she was a rabbit. "If you need anything, just ring the bell."

"Will do." He shut the door without another word.

Millicent turned to go back downstairs, but walked right into a mass of pink hair.

"Ah, hello, Millie. I didn't see you there," Delilah said, turning and trying to hide a large floating object behind her. By the tassels hanging down, Millicent guessed it was Clarence's magic carpet, rolled up.

"Delilah, what are you doing with—Oh my goodness! Is that Bostwick?" She ran to one end of the carpet, out of which Bostwick's unconscious head was sticking. "What happened to him?"

"He's just asleep," Delilah said with a casual wave of her hand.

"He looks really pale."

"It's the poor lighting."

"And he feels kind of cold."

"Well, that might be the effect of a sleeping potion I slipped him at dinner."

"Delilah! Unroll this carpet right now!"

She reluctantly did so, placing Bostwick's top hat on his chest.

"Where were you taking him?" Millicent asked.

Delilah sighed heavily. "Bostwick's right. You deserve to know the truth. We were going to Chiaroscuro."

"Bostwick wanted to go with you?"

"Of course not! Why do you think I had Dolly fix that potion for him? I said it was to help me sleep, you see."

"So much for the truth," Millicent said, repositioning Bostwick so he was in the center of the carpet, his head no longer hanging over the edge.

"I said I'd tell *you* the truth, not Dolly."

"So you were just going to kidnap him?"

"Well, when you put it like that…"

"Bostwick?" She patted him on the cheek. "Wake up. Please wake up."

"It's no use. He'll be asleep for hours, which gives us enough time to be well on our way to Chiaroscuro. Speaking of which, I really must be going."

"What's this about, Delilah?"

"I really can't say. It's a secret between me and Bostwick."

"Even if you can't tell me what you're doing, I'm coming with you." She sat on the carpet beside Bostwick, sighing in exasperation. "You know, he could have rolled right off the edge, the way you had him."

Delilah stood helplessly for a moment, then climbed onto the carpet on Bostwick's other side.

"Well, Millie, I won't argue with you. I've missed you, you know? Do hold Bostwick's hat, would you? Ahem. Carpet up, and slowly forward."

The carpet did as commanded, sailing out the window at the end of the hall and into the night.

Two

The Traveling Unraveling Drabbling Vanishing Carpet

Bostwick felt wind rushing past his face and heard someone talking, but it took a moment for him to be able to understand what was actually being said without slipping back toward unconsciousness.

"…and even if she didn't love him completely unselfishly, I think she would have eventually."

He recognized Millicent's voice, and knew by the "hmm" given in reply that Delilah was keeping up the other half of the conversation. What he was still unsure about was why they were sitting on his bed talking while he was asleep, and why his bedroom seemed so cold and windy.

"I think she really loved him," Millicent went on. "And if she hadn't died…"

"I personally blame that professor."

"Hollyhock?"

"Well, of course. Encouraging young impressionable children to perform black magic experiments just seems irresponsible, you know?"

"Yeah."

Bostwick finally blinked his eyes open, seeing a starry sky. He glanced on either side of him and saw Delilah on his right and Millicent on his left.

"Where are we?" he asked, sitting up groggily.

"The Wastes," Millicent said. "Only they're a lot nicer now."

Bostwick blinked a few more times and looked over the edge of what he realized was Clarence's magic carpet. He recognized the jutting black rocks and several piles of trash from his last time flying over the Wastes, but now these were surrounded by green hills and trees. Directly underneath their carpet, a flat black expanse of lake spread out.

"Heather did all this?" he asked, rubbing his eyes. "And why are we here?"

"We're going to Chiaroscuro," Delilah said, twirling something around in her hands absentmindedly. "Millie's going to talk to Sebastian, and I'm going to do… things."

"And I'm here because…?"

"I need your gallant heart and butler's loyalty!"

"She slipped you a sleeping potion," Millicent explained.

"Ah," said Bostwick. "I'm drinking from a flask from now on."

"Good, good." Delilah said, peering through Millicent's opera glasses. "Hmm, still no sign from Misha, but he must have made contact with Sebastian by now."

"Maybe they're busy trying to locate the bo—" Bostwick began, before Delilah slapped her free hand over his mouth, raised an eyebrow, then went back to twine her hands, and whatever it was they held, around each other.

"Shush shush, Bostwick. No reason to ruin our charming nighttime ride."

"Right. So are we just going to fly straight to the palace?"

"Hopefully, though I have a sneaking suspicion we won't get that far. Anti-aircraft weapons and all that."

"What?"

"Anti-aircraft weapons. My dad told me that Gremlins invented them, should they ever invent a flying machine. Turns out they're good for fighting off dragons. In any event, I'm prepared to go by land if need be."

"I don't think Chiaroscuro has anything like that." Millicent scanned the horizon. "They don't even have lights."

"You made them sound so advanced, though, Millie."

"They are, but at the same time, there are so many things they never had to deal with inside of a shadow. They didn't have candles or lamps, or glass in their windows. I'm sure they wouldn't even think of an aerial assault."

"That will be to our advantage! They'll never see us coming!" Delilah cried, throwing her hands above her head.

"What is that you're holding, anyway?" Bostwick pointed to the thing in her hands, which seemed to have doubled in size over the course of their conversation.

"What thing?" She looked at her hands in surprise. "Oh, it's thread."

"From what?"

Delilah pulled on the ball of thread some more, following the single string hanging down to where it wove into the carpet.

"Oh dear."

"You're unraveling the carpet!"

"Apparently." She moved to the side farthest from the unraveled edge, where loose threads already blew wildly in the wind.

"Maybe if we leave it alone," Millicent said, "it won't get any worse?"

Delilah placed the ball of thread carefully down on the carpet, but it rolled over the edge.

"Now it's unraveling faster!" Bostwick said, edging closer to Millicent as the habitable portion of carpet disappeared.

"Maybe if we stand up, there will be enough room for a while. Carpet, go down slowly."

They stood unsteadily as the carpet descended.

"We won't make it," Delilah said. "Time for decisive action! Millie, give me the hat, then kneel down and hold on!"

Millicent did as instructed, while Delilah turned to Bostwick.

"*Bost*wick! Catch me!" she cried, and leapt into his arms, causing him to stumble backwards off the carpet. The two of them fell through the air towards the lake below. She pushed him away just as they were about to hit the water and floated safely to shore as he made a giant splash. Millicent rode the rest of the way on the carpet, which disintegrated at the edge of the lake, dropping her lightly into the shallows.

"Thanks a lot!" Bostwick said, treading water.

"I had to keep the hat dry!" Delilah said. "Besides, we never would have fit on the carpet all the way to the end. And really, this is a lovely spot to land."

"It's a lovely spot to catch pneumonia and die!"

When he reached the shore, he was sopping wet from head to toe. Though the water was only up to Millicent's knees, she stumbled on the way out and fell face first, soaking herself entirely.

"It's freezing!" she said, wringing out her skirt bit by bit.

Bostwick agreed, grabbing his hat from Delilah and extracting a large purple cloth from it. He wrapped it around himself, leaving only his head and one hand uncovered, drew a triangle over his chest, and whipped the cloth off to reveal a mostly-dry set of clothes.

"You're still a bit damp," Delilah commented.

"You try vanishing liquid without catching anything else by accident sometime," Bostwick said, draping the cloth briefly over his wet hair and casting the same spell before holding it out to Millicent.

"I'd just mess it up!" she cried, flushing crimson and flinching away from the cloth like it might do her bodily harm.

"Ah! R-right," Bostwick said, realizing that there were several disastrous ways for the spell to go wrong. "Well, I-I can do it for you, then."

"Lovely," Delilah said, conjuring a glowing, warm ball of energy while Bostwick cast the spell and Millicent stared grimly at the ground. "Now that no one is likely to get pneumonia or die, let's set up camp."

"Camp?" Bostwick said. "What about the bo—"

"—stwick! Bostwick! Misha is taking care of all that for now. We really must sleep. I'm exhausted, and I'm sure Millie is, too."

"I'll be okay," Millicent said, "if there's some reason we have to get to Chiaroscuro quickly."

"Can't we just tell her?" Bostwick asked Delilah.

"Absolutely not."

"She'll find out soon enough anyway," he said, turning to Millicent. "The reason we're going on this crazy expedition is—"

"If you tell her my secret, I'll tell her yours," Delilah said.

"Mine?"

"About that little, black book. Heh. I can see the fear in your eyes now. Not so loose lipped anymore, eh?"

Millicent looked from Delilah to Bostwick. "You mean the Ruzicka poetry book?"

"How do you know about that?" Bostwick asked, cringing.

"I found it when I was doing laundry one time. You left it in your pocket. I didn't know it was supposed to be a secret."

"Well, it isn't really. I've just had some bad experiences when poetry is involved. But as I was saying—"

"Kobolds?" Delilah said, causing Bostwick to freeze.

"You wouldn't."

"Oh, I assure you, I will."

"That's hitting below the belt."

"It's your fault for being so mysterious. Most people—honest, forthcoming people—don't have these problems."

"Interesting, coming from someone who steals people's memories."

"That is true, Delilah," Millicent said.

"Why, Millie! You have cut me to the quick, though I do see your point. How ever did you find out about that anyway?"

"Sebastian mentioned it, and Bostwick told me what happened."

"Did he?" She grinned widely at Bostwick. "Do you want to hear *my* version of events."

"That really won't be necessary," Bostwick protested.

"But I thought you liked honesty."

"That's… This is different."

"Is it?" she asked, staring him down. "You're the one who thinks Millie oughtn't be kept in the dark, right? So why not confess what really happened, right here, right now?"

"That's okay," Millicent said, seeing Bostwick's perturbed expression. "It's not important. I mean, I don't remember it and—and really, Bostwick told me everything last night."

"So you don't want to know what caused all the trouble? What terrible thing was said?"

Millicent shook her head, but could not lose her look of curiosity. Bostwick was torn between wanting to just come out and tell her that during the memory debacle he'd found out about her crush on him—which would only lead to her wondering if her feelings were reciprocated—and sticking with his decision to keep their relationship the way it was so she would have no qualms about going to the Academy. Deciding on the latter, he turned to Delilah, silently pleading with her not to go on.

She raised an unimpressed eyebrow, saying, "Well, if you won't tell her, I will."

"Wait!"

"A garish affront to the eyes," she said, grabbing Millicent's hand.

"Wha—?"

"That's what he said about your beautiful dress, that it was 'a garish affront the eyes'."

"That… that's what you meant?" Bostwick said, relieved. Delilah nodded and patted Millicent's hand. "You're an idiot."

"How dare you, Bostwick! That is exactly what happened. I saw it with my own eyes!"

"You spied on us using the Domino, didn't you?" Millicent said, exasperated. "I thought I asked you to stop doing that a long time ago."

"Well, what else is a magical shape-shifting mask good for? Except for pulling things from hats. But all we have is a non-shape-shifting Bostwick, so I guess we'll have to make-do with that. Let's set up camp! You should find a pair of cloaks in your hat."

"That topic shift was just shameless," Bostwick said, tired of arguing. He reached into his hat and pulled out the cloaks, which were made of a thin, black material. "And these are for…?"

"Warmth. I wasn't expecting to fall into a lake!" Delilah added in response to Bostwick's smirk.

"Well, unlike you, I'm used to camping in the middle of nowhere. Here…" He pulled a pillow and several blankets of his hat, which he passed to Millicent.

"What about you?" she asked.

"I think I'll stay up. For some reason," he said, glaring at Delilah, "I'm not tired,"

"In that case," the queen said, "make yourself useful and collect some firewood. If I keep up this energy spell all night, I'll be exhausted. Ancient Styx magic takes a lot out of you."

Bostwick took his hat and walked off to do as she asked, glancing back every so often to make sure she wasn't doing anything devious. Though there were shrubs and trees dotting the landscape, they were all too green to make a decent fire out of. He had to travel far from the lake, south to where the grass gave way to the usual red soil of the Wastes.

He found one of the black, dead looking trees and experimentally tugged on branch, but only managed to break off a piece about as long as his hand. Realizing that he would be here all night if he went at this rate, he withdrew a saw—which he hadn't used since his days of sawing ladies in half at the Academy—out of his hat.

It still took some time to cut the branch up, even with the saw, and Bostwick found himself trying to remember what Millicent had said about a spell for sharpening knives. Of course, he reminded himself, it was actually Alistair's spell.

The branch crashed to the ground as Bostwick stopped sawing and stepped back to think. He had never given the spells in Millicent's books much thought until she told everyone about Sebastian's memories. As he set to work sawing the branch into smaller, more manageable pieces, he considered the sort of person Alistair must have been. When Millicent had originally told him about her magic books, he had assumed their author was the sort of person to cut corners—casting most known spells one-handed, and creating dozens more for doing everyday tasks more quickly—but not the type of person who would commit goblin experimentation. Alistair seemed to be a sadistic megalomaniac—he was probably even worse than this, considering that Bostwick had heard the story through Millicent's rather charitable perspective—yet he had been a student at the same school Bostwick attended hundreds of years later. Clarence had even used the basement laboratory for a number of short-lived clubs, Bostwick thought as he stowed the saw back in his hat and gathered up the wood; thinking about what had gone on in that laboratory, Bostwick was glad he'd never taken Clarence up on his offer to attend any of their meetings.

When he got back to the others, he saw that Millicent was already asleep. Delilah had been passing the time by changing the shape of her energy spell. She was in the process of turning it from a ring to a cube, but let the spell fade when she saw Bostwick.

"Took you long enough. Poor Millie fainted from hunger." She gestured to Millicent, who looked quite contented with the blankets wrapped around her, green hair falling over her face.

"I wasn't getting food," Bostwick said, arranging the pile of wood on the ground, then used a flame spell to light some of the twigs.

"I'm sure they have food in Chiaroscuro, anyway. Millie said she thinks we're quite close. So, here's the plan…"

"So you actually have one?"

"Quiet, you. The plan is thus: by tomorrow, Misha and Sebastian should have found out where the bomb is hidden. Once we get to Chiaroscuro, we'll have his sister defuse it."

"You think she'll know how?"

"Well, of course, Bostwick. She's the one who set it in the first place. And if that fails, we shall just ask Sebastian to use the Domino to turn into some kind of magical goo and surround the bomb when it blows up, or maybe turn into a creature that eats volatile chemicals. On second thought, he would probably be happy to just eat the volatile chemicals if we told him it would kill him."

"And if none of those ridiculous schemes work, why don't we just have Sebastian take the bomb through a hat and leave it far away from any populated area. Millicent said Misha told her about hats all over the Wastes, right?"

Delilah stared at him, then thrust her fist in the air.

"Brilliant, Bostwick! If my completely plausible plans don't work, we'll go with yours. We'll save the city, I'll tell the Chiaroscurans that they are safe and sound and Styxian, and then maybe, if I feel like it, I'll tell Millie that it was your idea that saved the day. I bet she'll be surprised."

She laughed in an unnerving way.

"You didn't… tell her anything when I was gone, did you?" Bostwick asked.

"I told her you're madly in love with her."

"What!"

"I'm kidding, Bostwick. Good grief. All I did was fill her in about the love potion."

"That's worse!"

"Shh! You'll wake her up! And really, I don't know why you're upset. She seemed genuinely worried about you. I tried to explain how frighteningly dopey you were, but she refused to believe it. Though she was healthily repulsed by the kissing incident."

"You didn't have to tell her about *that!*"

"Of course I did. How else would I explain the potion losing effect?"

"You could have just said it wore off. What is wrong with you?"

"Hmm… Is that any way to reply to someone to whom you are indebted for fifty years?"

"Fifty?" he asked, suspicious.

"Yes. Since you've been such a dear, not telling Millie about the bomb, I'll reduce your sentence to fifty years. That's certainly worth a few secrets, right?"

"Are you serious?"

"Of course I'm serious, Bostwick. But you have to promise to leave the bomb business to me, all right? I originally dragged you along to just keep me company and stop you from worrying everyone back at the castle. However, now that Millie's come with us, she will handle speaking with Sebastian, and you will go with her to defend her honor."

"Her honor?"

"Yes! You know, if Sebastian starts this whole requesting to be annihilated business, you have to beat him to a pulp since Millie's too nice to do it."

"Well, I can't guarantee there will be any beating going on, but I'll definitely be there to help her."

He turned to Millicent, asleep with a placid expression on her face, and wondered once again why Sebastian had thought she should be the one to cease his existence. Bostwick had no doubt in her ability to do the spell, but thinking that she would do to so willingly would be like expecting Delilah to be completely honest.

"How adorable," Delilah said, breaking Bostwick from his thoughts.

"What? Millicent?"

"Oh-ho! Is that what you were thinking?"

"No!"

"Sure," she said sarcastically.

"You're the one who said it. How am I supposed to know what you're talking about?"

"I was referring to your loving glance toward the girl who, during daylight hours, you are unable to confess your innermost feelings to. It *is* adorable, isn't it?"

"Would you give it a rest?"

"I'm curious, Bostwick. Don't you want to know what she said when I told her about your first kiss?"

"N-no."

"Aw, you're blushing! How cute. Well, you can ask her yourself tomorrow. We have a bit of a walk ahead of us, after all," she said, curling into a ball to sleep.

Bostwick passed the rest of the night placing wood on the fire and reading from his book of poems, not feeling at all fatigued.

"It's all thanks to that sleeping potion," Delilah said the next morning, wrapping one of the black cloaks around herself. "Now, Bostwick, in your hat, you should find Balder Spleenbeck's old blunderbuss, glued back together. Do summon it for me." He handed it to her, confused, but she stowed it in her cloak without explaining. "Millie, you can wear the other cloak, while Bostwick will go as is. Let's go!"

Millicent pointed to a large white shape in the distance which she assumed was Chiaroscuro. Delilah prattled on about having her own methods for getting to the palace, but Bostwick only half listened. He was trying to think of a delicate way to bring up the topic consuming his mind. In the end, he decided to just ask Millicent about it directly.

"Um, about that love potion…"

"What love potion?" Millicent asked, staring blankly at him.

He slowly turned from her to Delilah, who grinned impishly and shrugged.

"N-never mind. It's nothing," he said, quickening his pace until he was far ahead of them.

"Don't mind him, Millie. He's just brooding about some silly occurrence when we were flying around Ataxia."

"What did he mean about a love potion?"

"It was hilarious, but sadly I've been sworn to secrecy about the whole event. I'm sure he'll tell you all about it someday. For now, let us set our sights and minds on Chiaroscuro."

"Okay," Millicent mumbled. "Still, I hate being out of the loop."

They reached the outskirts of the city before noon, but found almost no people around. A few shadow goblins peered at them from the windows of buildings, but for the most part stayed out of sight. As they went farther into the city, the streets became livelier, with many Chiaroscurans gazing through the maze of buildings and walkways up at the blue sky, while others stared at the outsiders with curiosity and mistrust.

"This really is a magnificent city," Delilah said. "I'm glad it's Styxians who built it. Makes me proud, you know?"

"They're not exactly Styxian," Bostwick said, noticing a few nervous glances from the townspeople. "Don't you think we should be a little more stealthy? We're getting a lot of strange looks."

"Don't worry. This is the fastest way to get to the palace on foot. Why do you think I brought the cloaks along?"

"Yeah, because nothing says inconspicuous like wandering around in black, flowing cloaks."

"Oh Bostwick of little faith, our suspiciousness is an integral part of my plan. We'll get as far as we can like this, but when we're found out, then they'll take us right where we want to go."

"Why is it that that sounds like a terrible idea?"

"Because it is terrible. Great and terrible! You should tremble before the awesomeness of my plan."

"Um, Delilah?" Millicent said. "There's a Chiaroscuran coming toward us. I think he's some kind of official."

Sure enough, a tall, barrel-chested goblin in a red uniform strode toward them. He seemed extremely self-important, but lost the spring in his step as he got closer, eventually stopping five feet from Delilah.

"Outsiders," he began unsurely, "what business… What business do you have in the City of Light and Shadow?"

"Who wants to know?" Delilah said, sounding like she was enjoying her impudence far too much.

"Petri Villanelle of the Chiaroscuran Order of Law," he said, finally sounding authoritative, but weakly added, "That's who."

He stood there for a moment, as if trying to think of the official policy on dealing with outsiders. After a long silence, he cleared his throat.

"Y-you're not magicians, are you?"

"Nope," said Delilah, pulling Balder's blunderbuss from under her cloak. "We're bandits!"

Three

Black and White
and Dead All Over

"The guard responsible has been found and is in custody," a red-clad policeman told Sebastian, who sat with Alcea in the Council Chamber. The room was large and circular, with an arched roof held up by intricately carved columns. Sebastian was fairly certain that it was built in imitation of a drawing from one of the books Inez had given him, and which had subsequently been taken to Chiaroscuro by the Ancient Shadows centuries ago.

"Did he see Misha leave?" Sebastian asked.

"Supposedly, but I'm not sure how credible he is. He told us he let two people in to clean the Document Chamber, and at the end of his shift, when he opened the door to check on them, a giant spider came out of the room and attacked him."

Alcea laughed softly to herself.

"I doubt that he'll know anything else," Sebastian said, glancing sideways at her. "Is there any other news?"

"Other than the city being outside of the shadow?" the policeman said, staring out the window. "We're urging everyone to stay inside, but few people are complying. Not that I can blame them. Most of them have never seen the sky before."

"I understand. Allow them to leave their houses if they wish, but let no one outside the city limits until further notice."

"As you wish." He bowed and left the room.

As soon as the door shut, Alcea transformed into a kobold and flexed her nubby fingers.

"I didn't attack that guard," she said. "I merely walked out of the room in my spider form and he ran away. It was quite pathetic. Not that they aren't all pathetic in their own way."

Sebastian didn't respond. Alcea had returned a few hours ago, saying that she had finished her task of checking the palace and surrounding buildings for any damage, and since then had kept up a stream of derisive commentary about the idiocy of goblin architecture—mainly due to Chiaroscuran aesthetics making it difficult to tell the difference between what was decorative and what was structural. He almost wished they would just return to her cave in the Gammon Archipelago, if it meant having to hear fewer insults directed towards his people, but with Delilah no doubt planning something, he was glad to still be allowed in Chiaroscuro to help keep it safe. He only wished he knew how much Millicent and Misha had told the queen about the shadow goblins, but had so far heard nothing about either one of them.

Nothing, that is, until the doors burst open, giving Alcea just enough time to resume her form as a shadow goblin.

Two policemen shoved a slightly bewildered Misha into the room. He straightened up when he saw Alcea.

"Misha Morceau, sir," one of the goblins said. "He was taken into custody shortly after the city came into the light. Had these on him."

"That was yesterday morning!" Sebastian took the pair of opera glasses the goblin handed him and placed them aside. "Why wasn't he brought to me immediately?"

"Forgive us, Your Majesty," the other policeman said, "but with everything else going on—water pouring from the sky, roaring gusts, and sudden waves of searing heat, as well as everyone's general panic—I believe the order to bring him to you may have been overlooked. The Chiaroscuran Order of Law will accept any punishment you deem appropriate."

"No one's going to be punished," Sebastian assured them, trying not to show his amusement at this dire description of rain, wind, and mid-day heat. "He's here now, so you've done your duty. You may go."

The two goblins saluted, turned on their heels, and left. Misha, meanwhile, stared up at Alcea, slowly backing away toward the other side of the room.

"So, you helped that human escape?" she said to him, sounding delighted.

"I, uh… Did I?"

"Millicent, you remember?" Sebastian said. He was furious about what had happened, but he couldn't blame Misha. Even before he'd lost his memories, Misha had been trusting and naïve. Millicent had surely used that to make her escape.

"Oh, yes. Millicent. Um… so, I didn't help her escape, I

just let her out of the city. Yes."

"Styx Castle returned after you and Millicent left. Did you meet up with Delilah?"

"Delilah?" he asked, backing away even further.

"He doesn't remember anything," Alcea said. "It's too bad. I would have loved to thank him."

"Thank me?" He finally bumped into a column on the far side of the room.

"Of course. You let the human escape, and she's the one who gave the map to the queen. If it hadn't been for you, the city wouldn't be where it is now."

"Really? Oh, well, you're welcome?"

Alcea laughed again, stood up, and walked to the door. "It's creatures like him and his sister that I can tolerate. They're just asking to be used."

"Where are you going?" Sebastian asked, standing to follow her.

"You don't need to know. For now, you may go wherever you wish."

She left the two men alone. Sebastian held his head, not having slept in over a day.

"I hope I'm not too late," Misha muttered to himself. "What was she doing here, anyway?"

"I told you about our deal. She fulfilled her part of it, so now, I must fulfill mine."

"But the Styx mapmaker's the one who raised the city."

"You remember being in Styx?" Now that he thought about it, Misha's eyes looked less vapid, and he stood more resolutely than he had in recent months. "You got your memories back? But just now—"

"I didn't want to tell Alcea anything. And if she really did do her part of the bargain…"

"She orchestrated everything, and will continue to protect Chiaroscuro" Sebastian said wearily, and walked out of the room.

"If that's the case," Misha said, following him, "then I can't tell you anything either, because you'd have to tell her."

Sebastian understood the memory merchant's concern. The magic of the contract was in his body now. So far, Alcea had not enforced it, but he didn't know how strongly it would affect him when she did.

"I already know you went to Delilah," he said, ascending the staircase that led to his chambers. "The real question is, why did you come back?"

"I… I really can't say. I'm sorry."

"What about Millicent?"

"She's back at Styx Castle. I'm pretty sure she told Delilah everything. Sorry."

"Everything… about me?"

"About your suicidal plan? She's still against it."

Sebastian stopped walking. It took Misha a second to notice and slow down.

"She told you about that?"

Misha nodded, waiting for Sebastian to start up the stairs again. "She told me about all the memories you showed her. I guess I understand why you feel guilty." He flinched from the look Sebastian shot at him, but continued. "Still, as your steward, I can't condone that sort of thinking. And asking Millicent to do it *for* you was even worse."

"There was no one else to turn to. She knows Alistair's

spells."

"It still seems like an unfair thing to ask of a person."

"It doesn't matter either way. Millicent's gone. There's no way she would return to Chiaroscuro now."

"Of course she will! She isn't the kind of person who would just run away."

"She already did!"

Sebastian had said it more angrily than he intended and immediately regretted it. It was no wonder she had run after being dragged away from her normal life into Sebastian's guilt. Chiaroscuro had just been her prison, and he, her jailer. Nothing he had shown her, or asked her to do, could change that fact. "I suppose it was foolish to ever have expected her to help me."

"No, it wasn't. Why do you think Millicent left? She needed Delilah's help to raise Chiaroscuro. She was trying to save you from Alcea."

"Well… it didn't work."

"No, but Millicent couldn't have known that the contract would still go into effect—I'm not even entirely sure I understand how that all works—but the point is, she may have left, but she didn't abandon you."

They continued walking in silence. Sebastian was not used to being lectured, and certainly not by Misha. Still, what he said made sense. What Sebastian didn't understand were his own feelings of resentment. He had agreed to Alcea's deal long ago, before he had ever met Millicent and had a chance at ending his existence. But now that that chance had been snatched away from him—or perhaps the thought that he would never see Millicent again—filled him with a sense of foreboding.

"Where are you headed, anyway?" Misha asked when they came to another flight of stairs.

"I need to sleep, Misha. I don't know why, but suddenly I've been feeling more and more tired."

"It happens. Anyway, if that's the case, and Alcea's not around, then I can go—"

"Wait," Sebastian said, not sure how to put it. "Could you… keep watch outside my chambers? She doesn't know that I've started sleeping. If she found out—I don't know why, but I feel like she would start asking a lot of questions."

"But I really have to… do a thing… I can't tell you about. It's important."

"Please, Misha. You're the only one I can trust anymore."

Misha thought a moment, looking unusually serious.

"I have to go… but as soon as I'm finished, I'll come back. I am your steward, after all, and I'm used to standing out there, so…"

Sebastian nodded, then continued on alone, wondering what could be so important yet so dangerous for Alcea to find out about.

"Oh dear!" Dolly said. "Oh dear, oh dear, oh dear!"

"What's the trouble?" Clarence asked, peering out from behind a shelf in the library. "Did you find them?"

"No, but I found out where they are. This was in Bostwick's room." She held up a piece of purple paper for them to read.

To everyone,

Bostwick and I have gone to Chiaroscuro to talk some sense into Sebastian, and by "talk", I mean "beat", of course. Don't worry, Millie, I'll let him live. Anyway, we went alone, for various and sundry reasons that I shall not elaborate on paper. Suffice it to say, don't try and come after us. Emmaline is in charge until I get back.

Love and Chaos,

Delilah

"Why am I in charge?" Emmaline asked.

"Ah," Clarence said, "that's why she asked to borrow my carpet. I thought it was suspicious."

"That's why," she muttered to herself. "Do you think Millicent went with them? It seems so strange for them all to suddenly leave like this. It's not as if there's a time limit on immortality."

"Or *is* there?" a squeaky voice said. They looked to the doorway, where a tiny, two-foot tall Gremlin stood quasi-dramatically.

"A Gremlin!" Dolly said. "How cute!"

"This one isn't cute," said Emmaline, walking over to him. "What are you doing here, Spleenbeck?"

"Eh? Why, I was just minding my own business, taking a stroll in the gardens, when I found myself back here."

He smiled up at her, but Emmaline was not fooled.

"Let me guess, you came to loot the castle."

"Perceptive," he said with a shrug.

"Well, someone's been stealing things around here. Now that you've shown up, it's obvious who it was. Did being King of Catawampus not offer a high enough salary?"

"Sure it did, plus a lot of lavish praise and blind submission, but after a few days I found myself pining for my former life of infamy. So I came here to case the place. Didn't think it would up and move on me."

"Sorry for the inconvenience."

"Um," Dolly said, kneeling to be closer to Balder's level. "What did you mean by there being limits on immortality?"

"Oh, that? Nothing really. Just wanted to make a snazzy entrance. But there will be a limit for that Cure-a-Zero city."

"It's Chiaroscuro."

"'Course it is! And I've come to tell you, it's in danger. That's the reason Delilah left."

"She told *you* about why she left, but not us?" Emmaline asked skeptically.

"Ha ha! I used an ancient Gremlin spying technique! Yesterday, I was in the treasure chamber trying to pry the gold leaf off the imbrogliochord—a goblinical musical instrument, for you ignorant humans—when I overheard Delilah's conversation with the magician. She confided in him that someone was attempting to use stolen Gremlin technology to blow up the entire city!"

"What?" Clarence and Dolly said in unison.

"Are you serious?" Emmaline asked.

"One hundred percent. She no doubt went to defuse the bomb, which is an utterly futile mission," he said with a grin. "If a trained Gremlin isn't the one to handle it, it could—no, *will*—blow up in the defuser's face. We build them that way special."

"Then we have to stop her," Emmaline said. "Maybe we can evacuate everyone instead."

Clarence stepped forward.

"Well then, let's come along as well."

"You? Why?"

"For adventure, of course!"

"And to help," Dolly added. "I've been thinking a lot since that incident with the love potion, and I've made a solemn vow that I will use my powers to help all living creatures!"

"Plus, if we don't come now, there'll be some reason later on. That's how these things work out, so we might as well tag along."

"I suppose you could try to warn the Chiaroscurans about what's going on," Emmaline said, "while I stop Delilah from detonating the bomb accidentally."

"Don't forget about me."

They looked down at Balder, who was standing with his trotter-like hands on his hips.

"Why on earth do you want to come?" Emmaline asked.

Balder's mouth wiggled, as if he hadn't thought of that, but then became a good-natured grin.

"I merely want to stop Gremlin technology from falling into the wrong hands. I could try defusing the thing myself. I am an expert on bombs, ya know?"

"Don't remind me. Let's see… I suppose the fastest way to get there is by airship."

"Then let's go right away!" Balder squeaked and ran down the hall.

"You should follow him and make sure he doesn't try anything," Emmaline said. "I have to get something first."

She sped the opposite direction, leaving Dolly and Clarence to catch up with the little Gremlin, who was surprisingly fast. He got to the airship well before them, and was already examining the controls with the look of an excited child, even going so far as to climb up one of the ropes suspended from the balloon to poke the hanging chains and high-up levers. He began to chuckle grimly to himself, but stopped as soon as Emmaline arrived. She untethered the ship, hopped in, and got it airborne in a matter of seconds, with Balder observing every miniscule movement.

"This must be exciting for you," Dolly said, picking up her staff, which she'd left in the ship two days before. "I think you're probably the first Gremlin to ever ride a flying machine."

He grinned hugely and said, "And I won't be the last. Ahem, but onto more immediate matters."

"Right," Clarence said. "How shall we find the bomb?"

"Hopefully, with this." Emmaline showed them a small, translucent pink rock. "It's a wishing stone. At least, it's supposed to be. It may or may not have been partially responsible for me returning to my human body."

"I thought I was responsible for that," Balder said, hopping to get a better look at the stone.

"Anyway, I think wishing is worth a try, given that we really don't have a better option." She pointed the ship toward the Wastes, then took a breath and clasped the stone tightly in both hands. "I wish that we find the bomb in Chiaroscuro before Delilah does, and in ample time for Balder to defuse it."

"Are you allowed to add clauses to a wish?" Clarence asked.

"I'm not sure but—Look!"

Opaque splotches of black, green, and peacock blue

began to spread across the stone until only a portion of the original pink color remained.

"Did it work?" Dolly asked.

"I hope so. It didn't do that the first time. I guess all we can do is fly to Chiaroscuro and see what happens."

Dolly grasped her staff in both hands and hit it against the deck of the ship, declaring, "Hear me, Oh Wind! Be our companion on our flight and speed our journey!" which only served to summon a light breeze that was just strong enough to blow their hair annoyingly into their faces.

"It's all right. I think a large wind might make the ship more unstable," Emmaline said, looking back towards Styx Castle, and then to the south, where several domed buildings of the Capital were visible in the distance. "I guess Camellia will have to wait a while. Well, like Mr. Charles said, a princess's duty is to the people. That, and there's no such thing as false tea."

She turned to see Dolly and Clarence staring at her with raised eyebrows

"Don't ask me what that's supposed to mean," she said with a shrug. "It's a secret metaphor."

"For the record," Heidi said, as she and Misha scoured Chiaroscuro's lower levels for any sign of his sister, "I still think you're crazy."

"I hope I am," Misha said.

"I'm only helping you find Danika so she can have you committed."

"We probably should be."

"Speak for yourself," she said with a sniff. "I'm not the one dumping all my memories or going on about conspiracy theories. You do realize that if this Alcea person had Danika set a bomb for her—which I'm not saying Danika *wouldn't* do, but still—and then you did all that stuff like giving the Queen of Styx your memories and smuggling humans in and out of the city, wouldn't it have blown up a long time ago?"

"Danika said they were waiting to set it. And now that Alcea's contract with Sebastian has actually gone into effect, and he can't get out of it anymore, the ideal time to set off the bomb would be now."

"Whatever."

They had come to a particularly shady part of town—in all senses of the word—and walked past greasy eateries and walls encrusted with decades-worth of grime that had dripped down from the upper levels. It was here that one could acquire illegally-fashioned hats for personal travel, as well as other ill-gotten goods. Given Danika's proclivity for creating contraband concoctions, she was well known in the area. A few goblins pointed Misha and Heidi towards a food stall frequented by "that loony chemical merchant", and sure enough, they saw a slender shadow goblin with pince-nez glasses and disheveled hair leaning over a bowl of soup.

"Danika!" Misha cried, "we need to talk!"

"Hmm?" She turned, slurping a wad of noodles into her mouth. "Oh, Misha! The police have been looking all over for you. Are you in some kind of trouble?"

"We all are." He lowered his voice. "Listen, remember a few months back how you sold Alcea those chemicals?"

"Funny you should mention that."

"Funny how?" Heidi narrowed her eyes, finally ready to believe Misha's story.

"Well, earlier today Alcea showed up and said it would be a great time to finally set it off, since that way everyone will get to see it."

"You didn't…"

"Set it? Well, of course I did! What's the point of having a bomb if you don't get to see it blow up?"

Heidi flexed her fingers, fighting the urge to get them around Danika's neck, but settled on raking them through her own hair.

"Why am I friends with you idiots!"

"Where is it, Danika?" Misha asked. "How long ago did you set it? How much time do you we have?"

"Calm down! It's in a cave by the ocean somewhere. Alcea said we'll definitely be able to see it from here, though."

"Oh, *that's* encouraging," Heidi muttered.

"And I'd estimate the blast will be around twilight. For a bomb like the one Alcea had, Gremlins build in a timer to give them time to run away on foot if their hypothetical flying machine crashes, and you know how small Gremlin feet are."

"Then that gives us some time," Misha said. "Listen, I've got to get back to Sebastian, but you two, try and figure out how close to the city it is, and see if you can defuse it."

"I don't see why you two are making a big deal out of this," Danika said, finishing her meal as Misha left. "It's not like Alcea would be careless enough to have me set a bomb anywhere near to the city."

"Careless has nothing to do with it. Misha thinks she did it on purpose, to get rid of us and entrap the king."

"That's ridiculous."

"You both are, but for the moment, I'm going to side with Misha. Let's assume Alcea has ulterior motives—No, actually, let's assume she has the motives a normal person would have for blowing something up, i.e. killing lots of people, the most people she could. How would she do that?"

"Since we're being hypothetical," Danika said with a shrug, "she'd put the bomb in the very center of the city, since the blast radius would just about encapsulate everyone. But, like I said, it's out of town."

"Yeah, yeah. So the city center would be this way, right?"

They headed up to a region of Chiaroscuro colloquially known as "The Park", a large public area spanning several of the city's larger rooftops. It was devoid of any vegetation, which could not have survived centuries inside a shadow, and was instead comprised of winding paths, hanging mobiles, and sculptures made of metal and stone. Pools of rainwater had formed in some spots and the sun beat down all around. The Chiaroscurans had never built any shaded areas because they had never needed any, though several women walked under parasols which they had once carried merely for aesthetic reasons.

"Ok, this is roughly the middle of town, so... Huh? What's wrong?"

Danika stood, gaped mouth, pointing to a crowd gathered around a four-foot-around sphere with a patchwork of screwed together seams covering its metal surface.

"What?" Heidi continued. "I mean, it's not to my taste either, but there's no need to be rude."

"It's not a sculpture," she whispered through gritted

teeth.

"You mean… That? There? That thing right there? I thought it would be like the size of an egg! How did Alcea bring something that big through a hat?"

"Maybe it's… a different bomb?"

Heidi uttered an incredulous "ugh" then approached one of the goblins inspecting the sphere.

"Um, so, when did this, uh, sculpture get here?"

"A few minutes ago," he said. "I think a dog brought it."

"A… a dog? Like one of those animals humans use for hunting?"

"Well, I've seen a drawing of a dog, and I'm pretty sure it was a dog."

"Dogs don't wear clothes, though," said another goblin. "And anyway, I think it was summoned."

"The dog?"

"No, this ball. The dog-looking-thing reached over its shoulder and sort… brought the ball into being, like some sort of… dog-faced magician."

Heidi walked back to Danika, who hadn't moved.

"There, you see?" Danika said with a twitch. "It was a Gremlin that summoned it. Alcea doesn't know any Gremlins. I think."

"Who cares how it got here! Can you defuse it?"

"Oh, no. I-I couldn't possibly."

"And why is that?" Heidi asked, finally losing it. She grabbed Danika by the collar and yanked her head down so they were eye to eye.

"I'm a total novice. Once a bomb is set, a series of locks—built in by the original Gremlin technician who designed the bomb—make it almost impossible to undo. They design them that way so once an assault is called, it can't be called off, no matter what. And if we tried to cut it up with our shadow, that could set it off, too. We're… we're all gonna die!"

"Hey! Shh," Heidi said, eyeing the crowd who thankfully hadn't heard.

"And it's all my fault. I just wanted to see an explosion, but now it's gonna go off and it'll hit everyone in the city and we'll be black and white and dead all ov—"

"Shut up!" Heidi cried, slapping her. "We're not done for yet. Misha said help should already be on its way."

"Help? From who? Sebastian, or…"

"Even better. He said that he personally met with the Queen of Styx and her two magicians. If they can't figure out how to get rid of this bomb, no one can."

She held a determined fist up in front of her face, then shook it and smacked herself on the forehead.

"That is… if Misha actually met them, and hasn't completely lost it!"

Four

A Meeting with the Empress

"I ask myself," Bostwick said, as the policeman led Millicent, Delilah, and him through the streets of Chiaroscuro, "why did I even consider that your plan might work?"

"It is working," Delilah said proudly, as the policeman glared at her. Though he had captured them easily—slapping a pair of luminous green handcuffs onto the queen and Millicent before Bostwick could even think of reacting (either to the sudden movement or to Delilah's ridiculous declaration of banditry), and then onto Bostwick himself— the policeman still kept a wary eye on all of them as he marched them, chain-gang style, through the city.

"How exactly is this 'working'?" Bostwick asked.

"He's taking us right to the palace."

"We don't keep criminals in the palace," the policeman said

"I meant the palace dungeon, of course."

"We don't have one."

"Oubliette?"

"No."

"Birdcage-type-thing hanging over a bottomless pit?"

"We keep criminals in the jail, of course."

"Jail! Bostwick, can you believe that?"

Bostwick did not respond, as he was trying his best to pretend he didn't know her.

Even if they hadn't been chained together, he was certain trying to escape would be useless, as the metal of the handcuffs—befuddlium, the policeman had called it—apparently blocked magic, as evidenced by Millicent's mousy brown hair. Then again, even with his magic, Bostwick wasn't sure he would want to go up against a shadow goblin, given Millicent's description of what had happened to Inez. Their only option now was to let the policeman lead them further into the increasingly stacked-up city and hope some sort of opportunity would present itself.

Though the jail was not in the palace itself, it was nearby, nestled under one of the palace's flying buttresses. The building was solid and imposing, the roof adorned with a statue of a woman with a sword in one hand, held up to the sky, and a flail in the other, held down to one side.

"Impressive," Delilah said.

"It represents justice and punishment," the policeman replied, leading them inside.

Beyond the first room, which had only an unmanned desk, was a larger, stable-like area that was divided into a number of cells, each constructed of the green, magic-blocking metal. The only light in the jail came through barred windows, but it was enough to show that there were already some inhabitants in the shadowy portions of the room.

The policeman, who still seemed somewhat terrified of

the outsiders, instructed them each to don a wide belt made of befuddlium rings, then put cuffs of the same substance around their necks. Only after locking all of these restraints did he remove their handcuffs and usher them into the largest cell, which already held three prisoners.

"You'll be in here until we have a proper trial," he said, locking the door. "Um, given recent events with the city leaving the shadow, I don't know when that will be, but rest assured, justice will prevail!"

He left without another word.

"Sure it will," one of their cellmates said. He was a middle-aged Chiaroscuran with an unruly chin of white stubble and blue-black markings around each eye, giving him a perpetually sleepy appearance. "Chiaroscurans will get justice when Gremlins fly. But hey, you're not from around here, are you?"

"Not exactly," Delilah said.

"The name's Augustus Ekphrasis," he said, holding out his hand in a cordial yet lazy fashion.

"I'm Delilah Glossolalia, Queen of Styx, and these are my maid and butler, Millicent and Bostwick."

"That's fine. This here is Meg Ottavarima," he explained, gesturing behind him to a wispy young goblin who surveyed them with calm yellow eyes. "She insists she's actually the human Empress Hypatia."

"I once had a group of wretched goblins think I was the empress," Delilah said.

"Small world. So, what are you in for?"

"We impersonated bandits," Bostwick said moodily.

"That's rough."

"And you?" Delilah asked politely.

"The Empress was found wandering the palace, snatching up jewels and things. I, on the other hand, am a public menace."

"Oh?"

"See, it's law, or at least it was until the city decided to pop into the daylight, that Chiaroscurans stay secret. We can venture out in disguise and sell our wares, so long as no one knows what we are. Now I can see the reasoning behind this, as the Styx goblins would likely report us to the Empire, and we'd be shipped away and vivisected and whatnot. Anyway, I don't particularly care. I say we tell the world what we are and dash the consequences! So I took up a letter writing campaign to tell the empress about us and see if we couldn't work something out. Well, for public safety, my letters were seized and I was chucked in here."

"Just like that?"

"Well, I did do it repeatedly after being told to stop, and the letters themselves were not a little threatening."

"Still, you don't seem like such bad criminals to me. What about that fellow?" she said, gesturing to the tall, gaunt Chiaroscuran in the next cell over.

"Serial murderer. Known as the Candlestick Maker. Can't imagine why."

"All right then," Delilah said, scooting away from the other cell.

"Yeah, prison life isn't so bad," Augustus continued. "We get three meals a day and it's not like we were really free out there anyway. Although these make things a little annoying."

He pointed to the green belt around his own waist.

"Hmm, yes. But they could be quite fashionable, you know?"

Augustus nodded but said nothing. The only sound to be heard was a soft sniffling coming from the corner of the cell. This prisoner was sitting in the fetal position and was, apparently, trying his hardest not to burst into tears.

"Is he all right?" Millicent asked.

"Probably not," Augustus said with an apathetic sniff. "He's got it into his head that he was the cause of the city popping out of the shadow, and thus it will be his fault if we're all vivisected."

"Nonsense," Delilah said. "I'm the one responsible for that, along with my mapmaker, I suppose."

"Sure you are," said Augustus, then whispered to the Empress, "I tell ya, I'm the last sane one in here."

"But why do you think it's your fault?" Millicent asked, walking over to the fourth prisoner and kneeling down.

"Because I... I failed at my post," he whimpered. "I can't even spot an erroneous maid."

"Maid?" Millicent leaned in to get a better look at the prisoner, then gasped. "Oh no, it's you!"

"That's what they'll all say as they're carted off to the Academy."

"No. I mean it's you, the guard from the palace."

Though he was dressed in a white tunic and pants instead of his former red uniform, his round, youthful face was easy to recognize, even if it was blue and puffy from crying.

"That's me," he said miserably.

"But it really wasn't your fault! And anyway, I sort of tricked you."

"You?"

"I was the maid you let into the Document Chamber."

He squinted at her, then sighed.

"So you aren't even really a shadow goblin. It shows how perceptive I am."

"If it helps, I really am a maid. And Delilah really is the one who brought the city into the light. But we're going to make sure that everyone's safe."

"Oh yeah?" Augustus asked, crawling over to the corner to join them.

"I'm declaring you all full citizens," Delilah said. "That way, the Empire can't lay a finger on you unless they want to have a war with Styx."

"So you see," Millicent explained, "it's a good thing the city is here."

"That doesn't excuse my shameful cowardice," the guard said. "I deserted my post. Nothing can make up for that."

"What do you mean? Didn't you stay there the whole time?"

The guard turned around until he was fully facing the corner of the room, sniffled, then spoke in a muffled voice.

"I kept watch for several hours, but then I thought that I'd better check on you and the new guy. It was his first day, so I figured that was what was taking so long. Anyway, when I opened the door, a giant white spider—eight feet tall at least—came crawling out of the room towards me. I'm not going to make any excuses. I ran. I was terrified so I ran."

He said nothing more. Augustus muttered something to the Empress while Bostwick and Delilah exchanged a curious glance.

"This white spider," Delilah said, "did it have a blue hourglass on its body?"

"It did," he mumbled.

"It didn't talk, or anything, did it?"

"I know this all sounds crazy to you."

"Not at all. As a matter of fact, we have seen such a spider. And ours was *not* a spider."

"Yours wasn't… a woman, was it?" he asked, turning around.

"I guess you could call her that," Bostwick said. "Why? Did the spider change shape?"

"Well, I didn't see it happen, exactly, and I thought maybe my eyes were playing tricks on me but… after I ran away, I hid behind a pillar, and when I looked back, the spider was gone, and in its place was a Chiaroscuran woman. She was short and she wore a purple dress like a doctor."

"Like a doctor?" Delilah asked.

"Ah, outsiders," Augustus said. "See, in Chiaroscuro, most people just wear blue, black, or white. We have colors reserved for certain jobs, like red for policemen, orange for councilmen, purple for doctors, and so on. Comes from the colors the magicians used to wear to say what year they were."

"But the dress was kind of strange, too," the guard continued. "It was kind of cut like a nightgown, all made of silk and flowing. Not like the clothes we normally wear out and about."

"But that sounds like…" Millicent began, then stood up and crossed to the opposite side of the cell. "I think the person you saw was Alcea."

"So Alcea is an immortal beast?" Bostwick said.

"Great," Delilah said, "one more psychotic shape-shifter to deal with."

"What if she's the same one from the cave? She did like making trades, so that could explain her bargain with Sebastian."

"I don't have a clue what they're talking about," Augustus muttered to the Empress. "I liked prison a lot more before it got so crowded. Before they decided to turn it into a madhouse and a zoo."

"What do you mean 'zoo'?" Millicent asked, as Bostwick and Delilah continued to debate whether they were dealing with a new immortal beast or an old one, as well as which scenario would be better.

"They decided to bring animals in here yesterday, along with some raving lunatic, who has thankfully been taken away. I suppose the beasts are clean enough, but still."

He pointed to a cell across from the Candlestick Maker's. Millicent could make out two large, brown lumps but could not distinguish any features.

"What kind of animals are they?" she asked.

"I'm not sure exactly. Some kind of rat, I think."

At this, one of the creatures lifted its head indignantly and came closer to their cell. It had a round, whiskery snout and what looked, even in the dim light, like webbed toes.

"The capybaras!" Millicent said. "What are they doing here?"

"I lent them to Misha," Delilah said. "He must have gotten them confiscated and thrown in prison. How do you like that?"

The capybara snorted, made a gruff noise like it was clearing its throat, then said, in a deep baritone, "It's a good thing you're here, Your Majesty."

"It can talk?" Bostwick asked incredulously.

"Of course he can," Delilah explained. "He's just the strong silent type. Now, you were saying, Octavio?"

"Millicent, did you know they could talk?"

The capybara ignored Bostwick's disbelief and continued. "Have you found the bomb yet, Your Majesty?"

"What bomb?" Millicent asked. Receiving no answer, she ventured on. "Is that why we came to Chiaroscuro? That's the secret, isn't it?"

Delilah stared at the ground, opened and closed her fist several times, then shook the bars of the cell and thrust a finger towards the capybara. "You never say a word, never ever ever, and *this* is what you decide to blurt out? Honestly!"

"It's not his fault!" Millicent said. "Why didn't you tell me there was a bomb?"

"I didn't want to worry you."

"Well, I'm worried now! Where is it? How much time do we have?"

"I'm afraid I don't know. But don't fret, Millie. Misha has already led the way for us. The bomb is in the palace. We just have to find out which room."

Millicent scanned the cell, searching for a way out, then bit her lip; they were clearly trapped.

"Now wait just a minute," Augustus said. "A moment ago you were assuring us that Chiaroscuro would be safe. I don't think, with a live bomb in the city, that that's going to be very possible."

"Not while we're in jail, at least," Millicent said.

"My plan worked out better in my head," Delilah said, "but I was intending to escape anyway, so…"

"Good luck with that," said Augustus. "The keys are in the next room, no one's around to bring them to us, and none of us can use magic."

"You can't break down the door, can you?" Delilah asked the capybara, who shook its head.

"Then I guess we're stuck," Millicent said, sitting down drearily.

Bostwick looked around the cell for some means of escape, but the floor, wall, and ceiling were made of stone. He watched as Delilah reached through and fiddled with the lock on the door with no success.

"Wait a minute," he said. "You can fit your arms through there?"

"Of course I can, Bostwick. I'm doing it now."

"Can you fit the rest of yourself through?"

She tried to, but no matter which way she turned or how much she exhaled, she couldn't fit. "Perhaps I underestimated Chiaroscuran ingenuity," she said, sitting beside Millicent.

"What about you," he asked the Empress, who jumped, looking shocked that anyone other than Augustus would address her. "You look like you could fit through the bars."

All eyes were on the Empress, who stood up and walked to the cell door as if she were floating through space. She turned sideways and fit her entire body, which was terribly thin, right through the bars.

Delilah cheered as the Empress glided to the next room and returned with the keys.

"Good job, Empress," Augustus said as the she opened the cell door, "but why couldn't you have done that before?"

"You never asked," she said in a steady voice.

"I didn't know you could!"

"Of course I can. I'm a ghost after all."

"A ghost?" Bostwick asked. He took the keys and began unlocking everyone's collars and belts. Millicent's first free action was turning her hair back to its usual green.

"Of course," Augustus said. "Empress Hypatia Mbaga died two hundred something years ago. It would just be silly to think she'd still be alive."

"Imagining yourself to be a historical person, I've heard of," Delilah said. "Imagining yourself to be the *ghost* of a historical person…"

"Anyway," Bostwick said. "We should head to the palace."

"Right. But what about you all?" Delilah surveyed her fellow prisoners, then clapped her hands. "Ah, yes, you two are pardoned. As a queen, I can do that. Just don't do anymore suicidal letter campaigns, Augustus, and watch over the Empress. As for you—what is your name, anyway?" she said to the guard, who had neither left the cell nor removed his beffudlium.

"Cecil Roderick Fugue."

"Yes, well, you're pardoned too. And since you know at least part of the layout of the palace, I think you should come along with us."

"But I'm—"

"Pshaw! I don't care what you are, or what you were. Come to reclaim your honor and all that."

"Well, it is my job to protect the city. I'll do it!"

"Shouldn't you get rid of the befuddlium?" Bostwick asked, unlocking the capybaras' cell.

"I shall wear it as a sign of my shame," he said, sounding almost as self-important as the first time Millicent met him, "and of my soon-to-be-recovered glory!"

"Lovely!" Delilah said. "Now, Octavio and Bertram, you might as well go back to Styx Castle. You'd be no help in bomb defusal." The two capybaras grunted and lumbered out of their cell. "Now then, I guess we're all set to go, unless we're forgetting anyone?"

"What about me?" the Candlestick Maker asked in a raspy voice. "I have ways of, heh, persuading people to talk."

Delilah paused, looked him square in the eye, and said "No." She then spun on her heel and led the way out of the room.

Five

When Gremlins Fly

The airship did not reach Chiaroscuro until sunset. The buildings were cast in orange light, and long shadows spread across the rooftops and down into the city's lower levels.

"Marvelous!" Clarence remarked. "It's as if they took every artistic movement and combined them into one."

"It's a bit too human for my taste," Balder said. "Heh, look at them down there." He pointed down at a crowd of shadow goblins that was staring up at the airship. "They're trembling in awe at the sight of Gremlin technology."

"This isn't Gremlin technology," Emmaline said. "They're terrified of the ship because they've never seen anything like it before. I don't want to make a scene, but I don't know where we should start looking for the bomb. Should we just keep flying?"

"If I were going to blow up an entire city," Balder said. "I would put the bomb right in the center of everything, so the blast would destroy anything within the city limits. Heh heh. Not that I would ever do a thing like that."

"Of course not," Emmaline said. "I guess we'll head towards the city center, though."

Emmaline piloted the ship towards an open area of statues and footpaths. She would have flown straight over it, but noticed a blazing blue fire on the ground, which was the only light she'd seen in the city so far. A Chiaroscuran was beside the fire, jumping up and down and waving her arms. Recognizing this as a signal, Emmaline landed and tied the ship to a sculpture of a water lily. A small crowd of goblins stood at a distance, watching the outsiders climb out of their ship.

The goblin who had been next to the fire, a short, blue-black colored woman, approached them.

"You must be the queen's magicians," she said. "Well, the bomb is right over here."

She led them to a large metal sphere where another goblin—this one with pince-nez and black stripes running up her cheeks—stood by an open hatch which revealed a maze of springs, gears, and glass tubes. Balder trotted over to this and peered in, conjured a number of tools, then snapped his goggles on and went to work.

"Um, thanks for finding it," Emmaline said, "but who are you?"

"And I'm Heidi," the short one said. "And this is Danika, Misha's sister."

"I'm impressed that you've got a Gremlin on staff," Danika said. "The Queen of Styx must really be something."

"He's not what I would call 'on staff'," Emmaline said, noticing Balder's feet swinging out from the inside of the bomb, "but he'll hopefully be able to handle this particular situation."

"Oh, good. Because if this is the bomb I set, it's rigged to blow up in about an hour or so."

"If it's the one *you* set?"

"Um," Dolly said, ignoring this. "Whatever the case, shouldn't we evacuate?"

"The thing is," Heidi said, "according to Misha, Sebastian's enslaved to Alcea or something, which means she sort of has control of the entire Council, and the police force, since he's the king. I'm not exactly sure how it works, but apparently a magical contract is involved, so…"

"We also don't want to cause a panic," Emmaline said.

"You're telling us. A couple people already thought it looked suspicious, so we've been telling everyone it's a sculpture that Danika's working on." She held up her hand beside her mouth, whispering, "and she's just eccentric enough for people to believe it."

"Still, we can't let everyone stay here, in case Balder can't defuse it."

"Wait a moment," Clarence said, smiling widely at the crowd, which had tripled in size since the airship landed. Apparently, news spread fast in Chiaroscuro. "I think I've got a brilliant idea. And I do believe you'll need to play along for it to work, Emmaline."

"All right, but the clock is ticking."

Clarence waved his hand airily at her, then hopped onto one of the stone benches populating the square.

"Attention citizens of Chiaroscuro!" he cried. "There is no need to fear us. We are diplomats from the Empire."

This caused a great amount of murmuring, gasping, and pointing from the crowd, as well as a dirty look from one particularly scruffy-looking goblin.

"Yes, well," Clarence continued, brushing hair out of his face. "We have heard the story of your plight. A great wrong was done many years ago, and today, it shall be righted. As we speak, Queen Delilah Glossolalia of Styx is negotiating with your king. By the end of the day, you will all officially be citizens of the country of Styx!"

The reaction of the crowd was immediate. The citizens noticeably relaxed and broke into smiles, while several people who had been hiding inside buildings came out to witness the historic speech being made.

"Clarence, is this really a good idea?" Emmaline asked.

"Delilah already considers them citizens."

"Yes, but all this about us being Imperial diplomats?"

"Well, as a magician, technically that's what I am."

"I suppose so. Just… just don't do anything crazy."

"I won't." He turned back to the crowd. "Your citizenship, of course, is not the only thing at stake! When the empress learned of your existence and what had been done to your ancestors, she realized that a crime against goblinity had been committed."

"What?" Emmaline whispered.

"Technically the empress did say something like that," Dolly supplied. "The one Millicent told us about, who lived two hundred years ago."

"And that crime has continued to have effect for centuries," Clarence continued, "but that all ends today. Now is the time for Chiaroscuro to come into the light and for all shadow goblins to stop living in fear! Today, the Empire is recognizing you all as full members of the goblin race, with all protections therein!"

"Are you serious?" an elderly goblin asked. "I never thought I'd see the day."

"Nifty, isn't it?" Clarence said. "Now all we need to do is make it official by drawing up a treaty. Who will step forward to sign it?" He scanned the crowd full of smiling, though stationary, Chiaroscurans. "Come now, we won't bite."

"I'll do it," the scruffy goblin said, stepping forward. He was followed by a skinny woman who waived at Clarence like an old friend. Clarence politely waved back

"Excellent," he said. "You wouldn't happen to have something to write on, though? I seem to have forgotten the treaty."

"Of course." The Chiaroscuran handed him a folded sheet of paper. "Ignore the threatening letter on the other side."

Clarence pulled a fountain pen from inside his shabby hat and began writing a treaty as Emmaline glanced back at Balder, who was working diligently on the bomb. After Clarence had finished the long-winded wording of the treaty, he drew three straight lines at the bottom and signed his name on one of them. The Chiaroscuran followed suit, writing *Augustus Ekphrasis*.

"I've been waiting a long time for this," Augustus said.

"Now all that's left is for you to sign, Emmaline."

"Oh, well, all right," she said, signing the paper as Augustus held his breath. As she wrote the final "a" in *Camellia* and lifted pen from paper, Clarence snatched the treaty and held it above his head.

"It's official!" he said, and the crowd cheered. "Now, to celebrate this momentous occasion, let's all go out of the city, into the newly renovated grassy knolls of the Wastes, and have a picnic! Make sure to tell all your friends and acquaintances. Even the antisocial shut-ins should be invited. We wouldn't want anyone to miss out!"

Augustus and the woman with him shook Clarence's hand, then ran, with many of the other goblins, to go spread the good news throughout the city.

"And that is how we shall evacuate the city without causing wide-spread panic," Clarence said, folding the paper up and sticking it in his hat.

"That was pretty clever," Emmaline admitted.

"It's a good thing you were here to sign the treaty, eh?"

"Well, it's not like it's official."

"About that… Technically, all one needs to make a legally binding treaty between the Empire and another people is the signatures of a member of said people, a noble of the Empire, and a member of the imperial family. So the signatures of that Augustus fellow, you, and me—as I just so happen to be distantly related to the empress—would suffice."

Emmaline said nothing for a moment, then cried, "That is the stupidest law I've ever heard!"

"It was quite useful back in Melieh's day, when the Empire had to handle negotiations with a lot of little nations. They just never got around to changing the law, I suppose."

"That's the first thing I'm going to do when I get back to the Empire," Emmaline said, half annoyed and half amused. "Now, let's see how Spleenbeck's doing.

"I'll stay and make sure the evacuation goes as planned," Clarence said. He had already started to direct traffic from atop the bench.

"You know, Clarence is a lot more competent than he seems," Emmaline told Dolly as they walked back to Danika and Balder. The Gremlin turned to them and wiped his face, which was covered in dirt and oil.

"This is quite a machine," he said. "I think it dates back to the First Greml War. And the chemicals are quite the interesting cocktail. Fortunately, I've already made some headway. The good news is, I now know the size of the blast and exactly how much time we have left. The bad news is that that is not enough time to defuse the bomb."

"Then we'll be blown up?" Dolly said. "Well, the city's being evacuated; maybe we can get out in time. But what about Bostwick and—"

"This city isn't blowing up today," Balder said, buckling his hat beneath his chin. "We've got to move it."

"The city?" Emmaline asked. "There isn't time."

"What the…? Not the city. We have to move the bomb."

"What if that sets it off?" Danika asked.

"It won't. These were meant to be carried and dropped by Gremlin flying machines—which had not yet been invented, but we Gremlins have always been optimistic. See, that's what the handle on the top is for. Now, if we take everything out of the airship and have only the pilot inside, the ship should be able to carry the bomb far away from the city and drop it in the ocean. You!" He pointed at Heidi and Danika. "Remove everything from the ship. Dump out anything that isn't screwed in or nailed down."

They hurried to do so as Balder reached over his left shoulder and conjured a long, thick chain with a heavy metal hook on each end.

"But what if we can't make it that far?" Emmaline asked. "Won't the ship get blown up too?"

"If the ship is high enough up, then I can drop the bomb at just right time so it should blow up halfway between the ground and the ship, leaving both unharmed. I'll use this," he said, conjuring a small device that resembled a clock. "It's an altimeter. It'll tell me exactly how high I'm flying."

Balder ran to the ship, shooed the two shadow goblins away, climbed in, and hooked one end of the chain onto the rim of the ship's basket. Emmaline was about to get in after him, but he held up a trotterish hand in protest.

"The ship can only handle one person if we want to make any sort of distance carrying the bomb," he said.

"I have more experience flying."

"That's as may be, but this particular flight will take precision in reading the altimeter and knowing when to drop the bomb. If something goes wrong, that's the end."

"Spleenbeck…"

"You're a princess, even if you are a human, and a little girl to boot. It would be plain irresponsible to let you put your life on the chopping block." He straightened his goggles and zipped up his jacket, then turned away. "Just think of this as making up for trying to blow you to bits before."

"But—"

"And also," he said, handing her the loose end of the chain, "you have to be the one to secure this to the bomb. It's liable to slip if I did it. No thumbs, you know?"

He flew the ship up and over the bomb and waited for Emmaline to hook the chain onto the handle.

"Thanks, human," he said with a salute.

"Good luck," Emmaline said. "And… and be careful."

"Ha! Balder Dash Spleenbeck does not know the meaning of the word 'careful'."

The airship and the chain made a horrible crunching, grinding noise as they tugged on the bomb, but they eventually got the device airborne. The ship ascended more slowly than Emmaline had seen it go before, but Balder managed to get it high enough to fly over the city's rooftops by the time he left the square, and was flying a little higher every moment.

"There goes a brave little Gremlin," Dolly remarked.

Emmaline continued to watch as the silhouette of the ship grew smaller against the fiery orange sky. "Um, anyway, we'd better follow the shadow goblins out of the city, just in case."

By the time they arrived at the outskirts of the city, the sun had just set, turning the sky a dark violet. The shadow goblins had already set up stalls selling dessert crepes, tarts, and other comestibles, and a few were making makeshift lanterns and torches. Others had spread blankets out and were looking up at the stars, discussing the future of their city.

"You know, we'd all read about the kind of festivals the humans had," Augustus told Clarence as the magician purchased, with genuine Imperial currency, dessert for everyone nearby. "Of course, we never got to celebrate them in the open air."

"I guess this will be the start of a new tradition then,"

Clarence said, handing the Empress a crepe.

"I'm glad about the shadow goblins," Dolly said, "but what about Balder?"

"I lost sight of him after it got dark," Emmaline said. "He should be over the ocean by now. I guess we just have to wait and watch for an explosion."

"Explosion?" Augustus asked suspiciously.

"Fireworks!" Clarence announced with a nervous smile. "We may see celebratory fireworks, or rather, one big firework. They're all the rage in the Empire. Yes. You might want to tell all your friends about the explosion, though, so they don't, you know, get the wrong idea."

"How much time do we have?" Dolly asked quietly. "Should we go back into the city? Should we see if Delilah's somewhere in the crowd?"

"Have a crepe and relax. We'll just have to wait and see."

"I wish I could relax," Emmaline said, resignedly sitting on the grass. "I never really thought of Spleenbeck as anything but a criminal, and now he's putting his life on the line to save everyone."

"I'm sure he'll be fine," Clarence said, scanning the sky in the direction of the ocean. The Chiaroscurans were happily making up constellations as more and more stars became visible, but Emmaline couldn't think of anything but the airship.

Suddenly, the picnicking Chiaroscurans were lit up all at once by an intense burst of green light from the sky. They started to scream, but Clarence reminded those closest to him of the fireworks and they hushed. The sphere of light looked more intense than fire and crackled like lightning, taking up a large portion of the western sky. The shadow goblins stared at the burst until, seconds later, it burned out. The crowd gradually began the clap, and eventually broke out into full applause. After they had quieted down, Clarence told them that the festivities were concluded and that they could all return to the city.

Dolly, Clarence, Danika, and Emmaline waited until most of the crowd had dispersed before heading back toward the buildings of Chiaroscuro.

"Was it just me," Emmaline asked, "or did something fall toward the ocean after the bomb exploded?"

"It was the bomb casing," Danika said. "That bomb only destroys organic material."

"So it wasn't the ship?"

"Oh, well, it might have been."

Emmaline stopped to scan the horizon, looking for any small sign of movement.

"If," Dolly tentatively began, "or rather, when Balder gets back, he'll probably be looking for us in town. We should hurry"

"But he should be back by now," Emmaline said in a shaky voice. "The airship is practically empty. There's no wind. There's no reason for him not to be here unless—"

"Wait," Clarence said. "Do you here that?"

A faint hum could be heard from the distance. Emmaline held her breath and listened as the sound grew louder. Finally, out of the blackness, the balloon of the airship appeared.

"Spleenbeck!" Emmaline cried with tears in her eyes, as the ship flew in a small circle overhead. "Are you all right? You didn't get hit by the blast at all?"

Balder's gray face appeared over the side of the ship and looked down at them. He pulled his goggles off and grinned.

"Of course not! You didn't think I'd let myself get killed, did you? Never underestimate Gremlin technology!" He waved the altimeter at them, but it slipped out of his hands and broke on the ground. "Blast!"

"Everyone's going back to the city," Dolly said. "I'm sure they'd be happy to meet you, knowing you saved them."

"As I've said, lavish praise is not really my thing. I prefer fear and infamy." He disappeared for a moment and the ship began a slow ascent. "But I do have to clear my name," he said, poking his head over the side again, "as a Gremlin technician. Let the record state that I, Balder Dash Spleenbeck, absolutely could have defused and dismantled that bomb if I'd wanted to."

"What?" Emmaline cried. "Then why didn't you?"

"Why do you think?" he said, laughing as the ship climbed higher. "Thanks for airship, human. No hard feelings, I hope? Heh heh heh."

Still laughing, he flew the ship away towards the north without a second word. Clarence, Danika, and Heidi were stunned, while Dolly looked heartbroken.

"He stole it?" she said. "He's a thief? But… he seemed so cool and dashing."

Emmaline looked after the ship until it disappeared from view, then wiped her eyes with the back of her hand. For a moment, she looked like she was going to yell, but then uttered a small, strained laugh and said, "Did he really have to come back here and gloat?"

Six

Contractual Obligations

"Why can't you tell me what it was?" Sebastian asked Misha as they sped through the palace. He had just woken up when the sky outside his chambers blazed bright green, but whatever had caused the change in color had ended by the time he made it to the window. Misha seemed to know something about it, but refused to say anything.

"Because you'd have to tell Alcea."

"Was it something Delilah did?"

"Maybe… but probably not. So where are we going?"

"I need to ask Hollyhock about this."

"Who's she?"

Sebastian looked at him questioningly, then realized why he was confused.

"Hollyhock is Hollyhock's other name."

"Huh?"

"I can't even say it?" Sebastian asked himself, then addressed Misha. "That woman I made the contract with is called Hollyhock."

"I thought it was Alcea."

"That's her other name. But she told me to call her Hollyhock, so that's what I must refer to her as. I suppose this is the power of the contract taking effect."

By this time, they were walking toward the large rooftop terrace where Sebastian had first witnessed Chiaroscuro's entrance into the light.

"So how do we know where Alcea is?" Misha asked

"I can sense her," Sebastian explained. "Also because of the contract, no doubt."

They finally reached the open air and saw a starry sky above them. The terrace itself had fires blazing around the edge in a circle. In the center, a humanoid woman with a crest of purple feathers was swirling a ball of fire around in her hands. Her expression was haughty until she saw Sebastian and smiled.

"So you've finally taken your true form," Sebastian said.

"Immortal beasts don't have a true form." She tossed her fireball up in the air, where it vanished. "I'm sure you thought this was it when you were sharing memories with that human, but that isn't the case. Knowing the Domino of Nonpareil, it would appear that simply wanting to have the powers of an immortal beast would grant them to you. It's really something, isn't it?"

"So… what are you?" Misha asked, looking even more confused than normal.

"Oh, this?" She looked down at herself. "This is something that humans call an ifrit. They used to live in the Nopali Desert, though they're all dead and gone now."

She stretched out her arms to the side and flexed her hands, and the fires surrounding her turned blue. She then brought her hands close in front of her face and forced them towards each other, as if she were crushing the air between them. The fires, now glowing bright white, gathered over her head and joined into one large point of light that lit up the terrace like a miniature sun, which rose thirty feet, then remained stationary.

"There, now we can look at each other like civilized people," Alcea said, and turned into her shadow goblin form.

"Wait! You're Alcea?" Misha said, pointing at her in unabashed shock.

"He catches on quickly, doesn't he?" She walked to the railing and gazed down at the city with an air of annoyance. "They're all funneling back in. I wonder what happened out there."

"What was that light in the sky?" Sebastian asked her, looking at the city as well. Several people were carrying torches and lanterns, things which Sebastian had never seen in Chiaroscuro before.

"Oh, so you saw the explosion?" Alcea said lazily. "I've no idea how it moved."

"Then it was you? But what was that light? What was it supposed to do?"

"You don't need to know."

"Hollyhock! It couldn't have been something to hurt my people. We had a deal."

"We *have* a deal," she said with a smirk. "What exactly did the contract say I had to do?"

"You, the Second Signer, would bring about Chiaroscuro's removal from shadow and protect the city from all harm, natural or unnatural." He said the words mechanically, and realized that it was the contract speaking and not himself.

"The bomb—it *was* a bomb, of course—wouldn't have harmed a single stone in the city," Alcea said, frowning at Sebastian's horrified expression. "But I had to get rid of the shadow goblins… I'll have to do it some other way now."

"You have me, don't you? Isn't that good enough?"

"Nothing is good enough, Sebastian. Even if you have a treasure, if you aren't careful, someone will take it away from you. I'm just ensuring that you'll stay with me, and that you'll stay valuable."

"The Chiaroscurans have nothing to do with that!"

"No?" She turned toward Misha. "What do you think of your king, Misha? Be honest."

"Well, um, he's doing the best he can," Misha said, staring at the tiles underfoot.

"Do you admire him? Respect him?"

"Of course."

"You see," she said, addressing Sebastian once more. "As the ruler of a people, you are in just the kind of position that I don't want you in."

"What are you talking about?"

"Do I really have to explain everything?" she said, taking the form of professor Hollyhock. "If one girl's love for the *idea* of a Styx goblin was enough to bring you into existence, imagine what the love of your people would do once they learned about what you gave up to save them? It will be just like what happened to the Ancient Shadows all over again. They didn't turn out the way I wanted at all. I have to keep that from happening to you at any cost."

"That doesn't justify killing thousands of people!"

"It's the only way to be sure. It's not as if I like killing people, but they would eventually die anyway, so it's an acceptable price to pay."

"My people aren't part of some bargain," Sebastian said, balling his hands into fists.

"They aren't 'your people'. They're just mortals. Anywhere you go, you can find beings just like them; humans, goblins, even animals. The world is full of them."

"You sound jealous."

Alcea raised an eyebrow.

"As long as I have you, I'm not jealous at all. Although you do enjoy talking back, don't you?"

"I'm merely making an observation."

She glared at him, then shrugged.

"Maybe you don't understand the position you're in, Sebastian. I own you now. You're my possession, my creation. You owe me your life for the information I gave Inez and Alistair and you owe me your actions for saving this city. You owe them," she said, gesturing at the goblins below, "absolutely nothing. They're as far beneath you and me as mold is beneath them."

"Then why bother killing them? Most people aren't so vicious towards things they don't care about."

She looked up at the ball of light above them, so that the reflection on her glasses hid her eyes. "I really didn't want to do it like this, but you're being impertinent. I think it's time you learned about how this contract works. Kill Misha."

♠ ♦ ♣ ♥ ♣ ♦ ♠

The green light reflected in Delilah's wide yellow eyes as she stared out the Council Chamber window. They had been wandering the palace, looking for the bomb, when Cecil pointed out the window to the light in the sky.

"So," Delilah began as the glow dissipated, "so victory, I guess?"

"That was the bomb?" Millicent recast her flame spell which she had let die off a moment ago. "But it was so far away. And what was it doing in the sky?"

"Maybe it was supposed to fly over the city," Bostwick said. "I've seen a bomb that could walk on its own, so who knows what other kind of devices Gremlins have invented."

"And it probably blew up early because Gremlins are so bad at making things," Delilah said. "Well, crisis averted. I feel so accomplished."

"But why did these glasses show this room?" Cecil asked, looking into their pair of Millicent's opera glasses and walking around with his arm thrust before him. He had walked into several walls on their way up to the room already, but Delilah insisted on letting him use the glasses since he had better night vision than even she did.

"You're sure it was this room? So far the palace has seemed rather uniform."

"Not at all. The Council Chamber has a poem about Chiaroscuro, the City of Light and Shadow, written around the ceiling. I saw it when I was first sworn in as a guard. It was last week, so I remember it pretty vividly."

"And you can see that in the glasses?" Delilah asked, pointing at the ceiling, which had artistic lettering running around where it met the wall. "So they must be pointing up.

Which part of the poem can you see?"

"The part about 'Shadows living in shadow and hats within hats'."

"Up there." Bostwick pointed up behind the row of benches, then retrieved the other pair of glasses from table in front of them. "Why were they just lying here?"

"I don't know," Millicent said. "but if that *was* the bomb going off outside, and the city's all right, what do we do now?"

"We confront the bomber!" Cecil said. "Even if she is immortal."

"I think we should try to avoid her, actually," Bostwick said, "seeing as we have no idea how powerful she is, or why she tried to blow up the city, or even where she could be."

"Regardless, if she's a threat to the city, it's my duty to stop her!"

"Maybe we should split up," Millicent suggested. "You can look for Alcea and we can find Sebastian and tell him what's happening."

"Yes, you'd better inform him of the details. I, meanwhile, will be in the armory, and then hot on Alcea's trail!"

Cecil left them, heading in the direction of a small stairwell, while Millicent tried to lead the way to Sebastian's chambers. She was unfamiliar with the lower levels of the palace, but assumed that if they climbed higher she would eventually get her bearings. They finally came to the floor her room had been on, noticing the larger staircase that led up to Sebastian's chambers on the other side of the atrium, when Delilah stopped in her tracks and gestured out a window.

"What's that?" she said, pointing towards a bright light just above the northern part of the palace. "Another bomb?"

"But it's not going away," Bostwick said. "It almost looks like some kind of spell, but shadow goblins can't do that sort of magic, can they?"

"I know someone who can, as long as he's wearing my Domino. Do you think you could take us to that light, Millie?"

"Are you sure it's him, Delilah?" Millicent asked, leading them through a dark, windowless passage that went vaguely in the direction of the light.

"Of course it is. Since his people—despite their excellent night vision—are unaccustomed to darkness, he's turned himself into something or other and cast a nice little light spell for them. They shall hail him as a hero and he'll pretend to be a decent person, all the while slandering the name of Styx, no doubt."

Millicent was about to respond to this wild accusation, but the passage had opened onto a large room with several similar passages leading away and a tall double door taking up one wall. Light was visible under the door and voices could be heard on the other side, but they sounded distant and were hard to make out.

Delilah opened the door halfway and sped through, letting a shaft of light spill into the room. Bostwick made to follow her, but Millicent caught hold of his sleeve.

"I think that's Sebastian's voice," she said, trying not to sound too worried. It didn't work.

"Why don't you stay here?" Bostwick said. "We can handle it."

"No, I… I want to see him, but…I don't know what to say."

"You don't have to say anything."

For a second, she thought he was reaching out to touch her cheek—or maybe she was just hoping he was—but then brought his hand down to adjust his sleeve.

He cleared his throat. "Delilah and I will be right there. We won't let anything happen to you."

"It's not that," she said, folding her hands in front of her and mentally kicking herself for grabbing onto Bostwick like that. "I'm more worried about Sebastian than me."

"Especially if Delilah's gotten to him first," he said, and they proceeded through the door.

"What?" Sebastian asked, feeling his muscles tensing without his control.

"I said kill Misha. You need to learn who's in charge," Alcea said, looking over the railings again. "Anyway, he's outlived his usefulness."

"Leave him out of this!" Sebastian cried, but raised his shadow in the air and sliced towards Misha with it. Misha blocked with his own shadow just in time, then turned and ran straight towards the doors of the palace.

"Pursue him," Alcea said, without looking up.

Sebastian ran after him, trying as hard as he could to stop. He raised his shadow to Misha's waist level and cut sideways, but felt something block his attack. Standing in front of the astonished Misha was Delilah, energy shield conjured, with a look of contempt on her face.

"So we meet again, Tufty-Tail McWhiskerkin!" she said. "Attacking an innocent victim *yet* again, I see."

"Wait, Sebastian," Alcea said, and Sebastian regained control of himself and stepped back from Delilah. "I'm intrigued. What is the Queen of Styx doing here?"

"Apparently, I'm stopping people from getting chopped in half," she said, shoving Misha closer to the door. "I knew you hated Styx, Sebastian, but going after your own people?"

"It's the contract he made with Alcea," Misha explained. "It's not his fault. She's making him do it."

"The contract? But I'm the one who saved the city. Where is this Alcea person?"

Misha pointed and Alcea took the shape of a Chiaroscuran.

"Since my secret's out already," she said with a shrug, but suddenly she grew quiet and looked at the palace with a blank expression. Millicent and Bostwick had just stepped through the doorway.

"It's that human," Alcea said without emotion.

"What's she doing here?" Millicent said. "Sebastian, you don't have to serve her... do you?"

Sebastian said nothing, silently wondering why Millicent had returned, and why at a time like this.

"I've changed my mind," Alcea said. "Never mind about Misha. Kill the humans instead."

"You'll have to get through me first," Delilah said.

"Have it your way." Alcea nodded to Sebastian, who stepped forward of his own free will.

"Very well," he said, raising his shadow before him. "I've been wanting to do this for a long time."

Delilah blocked several of his whip-like attacks with her shield, then changed the shape of her spell into a rod and swung it towards Sebastian, forcing him to take several steps back.

"That's new," he said, swiping at her feet. She jumped and then floated easily back down with a smile.

"I've been practicing."

"Can't we do something?" Millicent asked. She, Bostwick, and Misha all stood at a distance, watching helplessly as Sebastian and Delilah countered each other's blows and struck their own with more and more precision.

"Human magic isn't designed for combat," Bostwick said. "I don't know what we could do, if he really does have a magical contract with Alcea."

"He definitely does," Misha said.

Millicent cast a brief glance at Alcea—who was not watching the fight but instead was gazing curiously back at her.

"Are immortal beasts dangerous, Bostwick?"

"The one we met in Gammon seemed powerful, but not violent—"

"You wretch!" Delilah cried, focusing all attention on the fight once again. The bottom of her dress had a large tear in it. She tore the lose material off and tossed it away, then charged Sebastian with her spell in the shape of a club. Sebastian stepped to the side and let her run past, then attacked. Delilah turned just in time to block with her shield.

"Why don't you attack me instead of my defenseless clothing?" she asked.

"I'd love to," he said, plunging his shadow down behind

her shield. She canceled the spell for a moment, stepped back, and conjured it again, so that Sebastian's shadow shattered the tiles of the ground where she had been standing.

"You don't really want to kill me?" the queen asked, looking at the smashed tile with wide eyes.

"I was content to remove Styx from its former location, but you had to bring it back. As such, I can't let you live being so close to my people."

"They're *my* people. And frankly, I've done a much better job of protecting them than you ever—"

The last word was obscured into a yelp as Sebastian's shadow grazed Delilah's shoulder.

"You're really serious about this!" she said incredulously, touching the cut and examining the blood on her finger. "You really *do* want to kill me. You ingrate!"

"Ingrate? Was I supposed to be thankful that you pulled my tail all those times, or that your family locked me away, or that they taught the humans how to twist magic."

"Idiot!" she cried, hurling her shield at him. He was forced back several feet, but managed to keep his footing. "I'm talking about right now! Why are you so blood thirsty all of a sudden? Do you want to make Inez's death worthless?"

He slashed down at her again, slicing a few pink hairs off as she floated backwards.

"Don't talk about her," he said in a low voice. "You don't know anything about her."

"I know what Millie told me. Her description was quite vivid. But you're thick, so maybe you don't remember what happened."

"I remember." He whipped his shadow through the air, but with less accuracy than before. "She died to protect Alistair and—"

"She died so *you* wouldn't become a murderer!"

For a moment, Sebastian froze as her words sank in. Delilah coiled her spell around her right arm and ran straight for him, mumbling something under her breath. Before he could react, she touched his face with her left hand, then punched him in the stomach with her right. She pulled her hand away and floated back to Millicent and Bostwick as Sebastian stumbled back, dropping to all fours.

"What did you do?" he coughed, standing.

"I removed my family's curse," Delilah said, waving the Domino of Nonpareil back and forth in her hand. "How does it feel to be back?"

"My true form?" Sebastian said, looking down at himself. Nothing had changed from a moment ago. "But I was already—"

"Yeah, yeah. The Domino appears when you take your regular form with it, which *was* a cat, until I uncursed you," she said, holding the mask a foot in front of her face. "I'd love to explain more, but I really must seal your powers until we sort out this contract. Besides, cats are easier to—"

A shadow flashed across her face, and half of the black mask fluttered to the ground. Where it had been cut, neatly between the eyes, blue sparks snapped, illuminating Delilah's dumbfounded stare.

"I'm not going back to that form," Sebastian said, raising his shadow in front of him like a snake poised to strike.

"Uh, Delilah," Bostwick said, taking her by the arm.

Millicent picked up the fallen half of the Domino and took Delilah's other arm, but released both when the Domino began to spark more violently. The piece of the mask in Delilah's hand suddenly erupted in a blue burst like a bolt of lightning which shot towards Sebastian and flung the queen against the wall of the palace.

The bolt of energy struck Sebastian in the chest and he fell, unconscious, to the ground. Alcea, who had been observing the proceedings with an aloof expression, stared at him open mouthed.

"Sebastian!" she screamed, running to him.

She knelt beside him and held his face in her hands, but he did not move. Looking around helplessly, she spotted Bostwick's top hat and snatched it with her shadow, then wrapped Sebastian and herself up in her shadow and disappeared through the hat before it touched the ground.

Seven

Hollyhock

Delilah blinked, surveying her surroundings. She was lying on a stone bench out on the terrace, where Alcea's light spell still blazed overhead. Three shadow goblins in trim purple tunics were staring at her admiringly, while a fourth knelt beside her and held a pack of ice to her head, which was aching terribly. After a moment, she sat up and saw Bostwick, Emmaline, Clarence, Dolly, and Millicent standing a few feet away, talking.

"So, what's all this about?" she asked, grabbing the ice pack and adjusting it.

"You hit your head, Your Majesty," one of the shadow goblins said. She looked older than the other three and had a black marking over half her face. "But you should be all right as long as you rest a bit. I'm Dr. Fugue."

"Any relation to Cecil Roderick Fugue, the extremely unlucky guard?" Delilah asked.

"Not closely, though I'm a friend of his mother," the doctor said, then paused as if considering what to say next. "We actually don't have very many surnames in Chiaroscuro, Your Majesty. They were instituted in the fourth generation, because names like 'Jasper, son of George, son of Sasha, son of Petri'—whose family line I and Cecil hail from—were becoming too difficult to manage. A number of arbitrary names were chosen and… But you probably aren't interested in all that."

"Sure I am. I am your queen after all."

Dr. Fugue and her fellow doctors looked at each other bashfully and the one who had been holding the ice pack said, "So you really do want us to be part of Styx? I wasn't there to see the treaty being signed; I could barely believe what everyone was saying."

"Treaty?"

"Ah," Clarence said, stepping forward. "The Empire has made a treaty with Chiaroscuro. I told the shadow goblins all about your plans to adopt them as citizens, though I left out the details. I'm not sure how goblins handle that sort of thing."

"Wait a minute," Delilah said, gesturing at him with the ice pack before hastily replacing it. "What are *you* all doing here? Who's watching over my castle?"

"Um," Emmaline began, not meeting Delilah's eye. "The capybaras are on their way back there right now. I'm sure everything in Styx will be fine."

Emmaline finished with an uncharacteristically enthusiastic grin. Delilah raised an eyebrow and Emmaline continued in a hurried voice.

"See, we found out about the bomb and came right away. We airlifted it out of the city, which is why it blew up in the sky. We saved everyone! Isn't that great! And then we saw the light coming from the palace and we rushed up here to—"

"Wait. Go back to the part about airlifting the bomb. You used the airship, didn't you! You blew it up!"

"No no. The ship is fine. Just fine!"

"So where is it?"

Emmaline looked to Clarence and Dolly, who nodded grimly in unison. "It's probably on its way to Greml, wherever that is."

Delilah leapt off the bench to throttle Emmaline, then swayed in place. One of the doctors kept her from toppling over and led her back to the bench.

"What exactly did I hit my head on? And who took my ship?"

"Balder Spleenbeck took it," Dolly said. "I already wrote a letter explaining everything and sent it to your father via carrier pigeon. I used magic to make sure it could find its way."

"And you hit your head on the palace wall when Sebastian cut the Domino," Bostwick explained. "Any of this ring any bells?"

"Right, Right. Well, we'll have to declare war on Greml at a later date. Anyway, where's Sebastian?"

"He got knocked out when the Domino zapped him," Bostwick said, glancing at Millicent, who was staring blankly at the ground. "Alcea took him through my hat."

"Well, I'm glad the Domino got in at least one good punch before it went down. May I see your hat, Bostwick?"

When he handed it to her, she examined every side of it thoughtfully, then punched through the top with a snarl. She was already tearing through one side, using her teeth to help, before Bostwick seized the hat back from her.

"What is wrong with you?" he yelled.

"Nothing at all," Delilah said, perfectly calm. She then addressed the doctors, who looked horrified at her behavior. "Are there any more top hats in Chiaroscuro, hmm? I think you'd better go destroy them. The safety of the city is at stake."

The two doctors standing on either side of Dr. Fugue went to do as requested, while Bostwick continued to protest.

"You didn't have to ruin *my* hat."

"Any hat can be used as a portal, Bostwick. And besides, you've been needing a new one for ages."

"But all of my props were in there!"

"I'm sure you can access them from elsewhere. Honestly, all this business with shadows and whatnot has proved that there is more to hat magic than meets the eye. For now, we need to keep Alcea and Sebastian at bay, which means destroying their easy access to the city. So tear up the rest of it, Bostwick. Do yours too, Clarence."

Clarence conjured a dagger and began cutting the already threadbare seams of his hat. He froze, removed his jackalope, Jill, from inside, and finished the job.

"Just in case," he said, patting Jill on the back, then handed his knife to Bostwick, who reluctantly finished the cut Delilah had started.

"Of course, now we'll have no way to follow Alcea," Bostwick said.

"About that," said Misha, stepping through the doorway of the palace, followed by a female Chiaroscuran with similar markings. "I don't think we can do it. There's no way to tell where someone's going when they use a hat, and if Alcea does live in the Gammon Archipelago," he said, glancing at Bostwick, "then it's too far for a mortal shadow goblin to travel."

"So you still think she's that particular immortal beast, eh, Bostwick?" Delilah asked. "Do we have any way of knowing one way or another?"

Misha handed her an old, yellow-green book. It was open to a page that had the words *Immortal Beasts* at the top, followed by two pages of text and pictures. On the first page was a sketch of a lizard next to a bugbear next to a human, with arrows pointing between them, emphasizing the fact that all three represented a single immortal beast, as well as a smaller sketch of a humanoid hand pressed against the forehead of a Gremlin. On the opposite page was a drawing of a woman with purple skin and feathers for hair. The haughty face was unmistakably that of the beast that they had met in the Archipelago.

"*Flora, Fauna, and Fungi of the Goblin Realm*," Delilah read, glancing at the cover of the book before returning to the entry on immortal beasts. "Well, this is definitely our beast, but is it Alcea?"

"She looked exactly like that before you arrived," Misha said. "She did all this stuff with fire, then changed into a shadow goblin, and then into a human. I'm sure that she's the beast in the drawing."

"What does the book say about her?" Emmaline asked.

"'I have chosen to include,'" Delilah began, then held the book out in front of her. "Ugh, my head hurts too much for this. Bostwick, you read it."

He took the book from her and scanned the page.

"'I have chosen to include immortal beasts under "Fauna", though I do not suppose they are exactly what we would consider animals. Little is known about these rare creatures, though there has been some consensus among goblin scholars. The beasts have a fluid, or potential, form which gives them the ability to change shape. Some legends hold that the beasts can share their thoughts merely by touching another creature, though why they would want to is anyone's guess. It is also believed that they do not age, nor reproduce. Whether they can be killed by anything is doubtful, and whether or not they can feel pain is up for grabs as well. Information on these creatures is hard to come by, and when found is too vague to matter. It would seem that the beasts want to keep it that way.'"

"That's not very helpful," Emmaline said.

"There's more. 'But what kind of writer would I be if I left it at that? Immortal beasts may not want to be found, but I've managed to track down a few on my travels. There are some whose identities I will not reveal, as they seem to be peacefully going about their business. The above beast, however, was just too interesting to keep secret. I sketched her in the most flattering light, though she transformed about a dozen times during my interview with her. Fond of the changing tides of the ocean, she can be found wandering the shore, trying to take unsuspecting travelers by surprise. She appears to have a mania for bargains, and only agreed to sit for my sketch when I gave her half of my prized Aureate Porcelain tea set. I must tell you to avoid her, should you meet her, and not listen to anything she says, in case you end up selling members of your family to her by mistake, which has happened before, according to her. She seemed quite proud of it.' That's the end of the entry," he said, handing the book to Emmaline.

"That… does sound pretty bad," said the Chiaroscuran standing next to Misha.

"Who are *you*, anyway?" Delilah asked

"I'm Misha's sister, Danika. I've also met Alcea."

"Ah yes. You agreed to set up the bomb."

Danika coughed into her fist, glancing sideways at the doctors, who seemed confused by everything that was being said. Delilah told them that she was feeling better and asked them to go inside. When they had done so, Danika continued.

"I only agreed to it because I thought she was a Gremlin enthusiast like me. I never would have thought she was an immortal beast."

"Had she only been a shadow goblin, that wouldn't necessarily excuse anything."

"On the contrary, a shadow goblin never could have pulled something as massive as that bomb through a hat. As far as I knew, the bomb was located safe and sound in a cave by the seashore, far from the city as possible. Now that I think about it, it probably could have been the cave you all found in the Gammon Archipelago."

"Was it full of treasure?"

"Well, yeah, but since none of it was from Greml, I didn't really take an interest."

"Then I guess that settles it," Delilah said with a sigh. "We can assume she is indeed that creepy shut-in from Gammon. So… now what?"

"It seems like Chiaroscuro is safe for the time being," Emmaline said. "I think we should probably stay here for a while and figure things out."

"But what about Sebastian?" Millicent asked.

"What about him?" Delilah asked.

"Well, the way he collapsed... I think he's mortal now."

"I think so, too," Emmaline said. "He's probably been that way for a while. Going from Professor Hollyhock's theory, it probably happened when he told you about wanting to be destroyed. When you refused, and decided you wanted him to exist for his own sake, that was the type of absolute love required to bring him fully into existence."

"But that means he doesn't need *magic* to kill himself anymore, so..."

"Nonsense!" Delilah said. "I'm sure Alcea would never allow him to do a thing like that. She seems to want him around for some inexplicable reason."

"Ohhh..." Misha smacked his fist down into his palm. "I think understand. That's what she was talking about before."

"Who?"

"Alcea. She wanted to kill us Chiaroscurans so we couldn't love Sebastian and turn him mortal. That's what she meant by keeping him valuable."

"So she only cares about him as long as he's immortal?" Emmaline said. "Still, I doubt that she'll let him out of his contract just because he can die. We might have to get him away from her by force."

"How exactly would we do that?" Bostwick asked. "We know nothing about immortal beasts besides the fact that that they can't die. How are we supposed to fight one?"

"Well… I don't know, but we have plenty of time to find out. Right now, however, I think the Chiaroscurans are owed some explanations, especially from their queen."

As the others discussed what to tell the Council and what to keep concealed, and Delilah demanded that the first priority was how to acquire something for dinner, Millicent looked to the spot where Sebastian had fallen.

"I guess he'll be all right for now," she mumbled.

"Don't worry," Misha said, "Alcea said Sebastian is her creation. She won't let him hurt himself."

"She didn't create him," she said, confused. "The students at the Academy did."

"Right, but…" He tried to recall what Alcea had said before. "I think she told them how to do it."

"That was Professor Hollyhock."

"Yes, she… wait," he said, putting it together. "Alcea… Alcea *is* Hollyhock!"

"What!"

Before Misha could explain, the door to the palace burst open and Cecil ran through it, carrying a sword in one hand and a shield made of befuddlium in the other.

"I'm here, Your Majesty!" he panted, leaning on the door frame. "Where's the immortal beast!"

"You're a little late," Bostwick said. "She already left."

Cecil dropped the shield and sank to the ground, muttering something about "not getting away with this."

"You were about to say something, Millie?" Delilah said.

"About Professor Hollyhock," Millicent said, "or rather Alcea, or, well… if they're the same person… If Hollyhock was an immortal beast, what does that mean?"

♠ ♦ ♣ ♥ ♣ ♦ ♠

Sebastian regained consciousness seconds after he and Alcea materialized in her shadowy, treasure-filled cave in the Gammon Archipelago. He sat up stiffly, taking in the fires that flickered around the room, throwing orange light onto the damp stone roof and the items of gold and silver that littered the floor. At first, he only heard Alcea's slow, angry breathing but could not locate her, then he spotted a fluffy white cat perched on the stones steps that led up to the mermaid's scale.

"So, we've finally come here," Sebastian said.

"I had to get you away from there. Your potential existence is still somewhat dependent on magic, and magic is affected by distance."

Sebastian had no idea what she was talking about, so he continued with his question.

"Are we staying here permanently?"

Alcea squinted at him before speaking.

"Have you ever fallen asleep before?" she said in a deliberately calm voice.

The question caught Sebastian off guard. He had been asleep a moment ago, now that he thought about it. It was different from his first few experiences with sleep, he thought, because it had happened so suddenly. And he felt a strange soreness in his chest from where the Domino's magic had struck him.

"Answer me, Sebastian."

"I have."

"Have you ever eaten anything?"

He couldn't tell if the contract was making him speak or if he was doing so freely. He personally didn't feel as if his answer was of much importance, yet something told him that Alcea would be furious if she knew.

"And I mean," she added, fixing him with her steady blue cat's eyes, "have you eaten since Inez died?"

"Yes."

She made the low moaning noise that any angry cat would make, whisked across the room and stood before him as a Styx goblin. Grabbing his jaw with her long-fingered hand, she asked, "And have you ever, *ever* bled?"

"No," he answered without hesitation.

She released him and seemed to grow still for a moment, before slamming her fist into a brass-framed standing mirror. Where blood would have welled on any ordinary person, Alcea's arm seemed to shimmer as if Sebastian were seeing her through a wave of hot air, then returned to normal. Small shards of broken mirror fell to the floor where Alcea unceremoniously ground them into the stone with her foot.

"It's happening," she growled through clenched teeth. "We have to stop it!"

"You don't think I'm mortal?" Sebastian asked with surprise. It had never occurred to him that he could become mortal after what he'd done.

"Not yet. Not yet!" Alcea shrieked, grabbing a copper vase and hurling it across the room. "It's just like last time! All my other creations got taken away!"

"You mean the Ancient Shadows?"

She glowered at him, her face looking uncomfortably like Delilah's, though he had never seen Delilah with such a miserable expression.

"After the Academy, I gave up on shadow goblins as a failed experiment," she said quietly. "I assumed that… that I was wrong about my theory that I could create a new immortal beast, but when I saw you on the sea shore, and I learned what you were, it proved that I was right. You were the only one who worked, the only one who survived, who's worth anything, and someone is still trying to take you away from me."

"But I'm under a contract with you." Though he hated Alcea, the look on her face almost made him want to comfort her. Her expression was like that of a petulant, though heartbroken, child.

"What good will that do if you become mortal?" she asked. "I've made contracts before. I've made thousands of bargains and trades with mortals because there are thousands and thousands and thousands of mortals to trade with. They're all the same. You're the only one who's really mine. I made you. I *created* you. One immortal beast produced another. Can any of the others say the same?"

Sebastian wanted to tell her, yet again, that she really had nothing to do with it, that the students at the Academy were responsible for his existence even though she had given them the information of how to do it. But he held his tongue. If he said anything against her, there was no telling what she might do. Now she was taking shallow breaths, though he knew she didn't need to breathe, and had sunk to the ground next to the tunnel leading out of her cave.

"It isn't fair," she said. "It isn't fair! Why are we the only ones who have to sit and watch everything go by? Why are we forced to be collectors and collectors only?"

"It that how all immortal beasts behave?"

She looked up at him, her eyes wide, her expression unhinged.

"We have our 'hobbies', as some would say. We like *things*."

"But you resent the creatures who make them?"

He thought of how Alcea must have felt at the Academy, lecturing students on how to do what she could not. She must have resented Alistair for his success, and hated Inez for almost turning Sebastian, too, into a 'failed experiment'. It seemed obvious now. Sebastian bitterly wondered how pleased Alcea had been when she learned of Inez's death.

"I wouldn't say that." She took the shape of a shadow goblin and stood. "It's easy to use them, after all. Easy to get them to twist their gifts because they don't really understand them. Do you think Alistair or any of the others really thought about what they were doing? At least you and I are gifted with intelligence."

"Inez was intelligent," Sebastian said impudently.

Alcea glared at him for a moment, then shifted her gaze to his body.

"You're still wearing that gaudy thing?" she asked. "Take that coat off, Sebastian. You're not Inez's doll anymore."

He removed the coat as she asked, then, having no further instructions, laid it over the top of the broken mirror.

Alcea breathed heavily once again, commanded Sebastian to stay inside, turned into a large, brown bat and flew down the dark passage out of the cave.

Sebastian sat on a heavy wooden chair that had somehow

survived centuries of sea air, and contemplated everything Alcea had said. Inhaling and feeling the slight ache in his chest, he opened the first few buttons of his tunic and looked down. There was a spidery, black and blue patch of inflamed skin over his sternum where he had been struck. He had never bled, it was true, never even had a bruise, yet here was a mark that had lasted, proving that he had once been harmed. In all likelihood, it meant he was mortal.

He glanced at the mouth of the tunnel to be sure he was alone, then looked quickly around the cave. There were a few maces and swords, but they all seemed too sinister, too violent. Finally, Sebastian's eyes lighted on a small knife that sat nestled between a glass jar and an old tea set on the stone platform that had the map of Ataxia carved into it. He walked over to the platform and picked up the knife in his hands. The handle was made of some sort of bone with twisting vines etched into it, and the blade was polished to perfection, reflecting his own pale face.

He held the knife up, wondering where to do it, how to finally end his suffering. He no longer had to depend on Millicent, who would never have helped him anyway.

But she came back, he thought. She ran when she learned of his plan, but she had returned. She had come to convince him to change his mind, no doubt.

"She just doesn't understand," he said aloud, holding up his arm. He examined the thin blue veins running just beneath his skin. "She brought Delilah with her, after all."

He held the knife several inches over his arm, but found he could bring it no closer. He wanted peace and silence and an end to all of his regret and guilt, but the only thing filling his head was Delilah's voice saying, "She died so you wouldn't become a murderer."

She's mistaken, he told himself, *as usual*. Inez had not planned to die; she was protecting Alistair. Her death was an accident. But then, it was because of her that Sebastian didn't have Alistair's death on his conscience, even though he had intended to carry through with it at the time. He knew now, after Inez's death, what it was like to take a life. But he would never know what it was like to murder. Inez had, indeed, given him that.

He looked at the firelight reflected in the blade and at his arm again. A single cut might do it. He could almost picture blood, his life, flowing out of him. Could he just throw that away, after what Inez had done for him? Was that any different from murder?

He tucked the knife into his pocket, still unsure of what to do, and heard movement behind him. Alcea had returned to the cave as Hollyhock.

"Come away from that tea set," she said, sounding unnaturally calm.

He sat back in the chair and rested his head on his hand, but Alcea lifted his chin up and looked at him.

"Answer my questions, Sebastian. That human who keeps showing up, the one you like so much, who is she?"

"Her name is Millicent," he said simply, but he felt the magic of the contract compelling him to say more.

Alcea walked behind his chair. He was certain that she'd changed shape by now, but he didn't bother turning around.

"I see," she said. "When I first saw her, she was disguised as a shadow goblin due to an illusory spell. I can assume she is a magician, yes?"

"Yes."

"And why did you bring a magician to Chiaroscuro, Sebastian? What were you planning?"

"She learned magic from a book Alistair wrote," he said, horrified by the words coming out of his mouth. He wanted to stop, tried to force his mouth shut, but still heard himself speak. "She knew the spell to make shadows disappear. I was going to have her to use it on me."

"Why would you want that?" she hissed.

"I didn't want to live anymore, after what I'd done. And moreover, I didn't want to serve you."

Sebastian briefly saw a scaly tail and assumed Alcea had turned into a wyrm. He felt hot breath on his back and heard the clink of her claws on metal, but in a moment she walked around to face him as the professor once more.

"But you're still alive, aren't you," she said, gazing at him with half-lidded eyes. "Why is that?"

"Millicent refused to help me."

"Why?"

"I'm not sure. I suppose it was foolish to ever expect her to. She seemed horrified at the idea." Alcea stared past Sebastian for a moment, then her eyes locked onto his. "You aren't planning on doing something to her? She has nothing to do with you. She isn't part of this."

"Do you think she cares what happens to you, Sebastian?"

"Yes. She… she's probably worried… about me."

"Then she is part of this."

"You don't mean…"

"If she loves you, then she's a threat to your immortality."

"You can't be sure it's her… Killing her won't change anything."

"There's only one way to find out," she said, changing into her shadow goblin form and grabbing a top hat from a stone table.

Sebastian had no time to think, or deliberate, or even regret what he was about to do. He merely took the knife from his pocket, held his arm up for Alcea to see, and stabbed the blade into his wrist.

Alcea's mouth had fallen open and she said something, but he didn't hear her through the agony slicing through his mind. Blue blood poured from the wound and splattered on the cave floor, and Sebastian was sure he would sink to the ground from the pain, but he didn't move. He couldn't move.

"Hold your arm still," Alcea said, and he did so. She changed into Hollyhock as she placed a small metal box over his arm, moved her hands over it, and removed it. His wrist was still dripping with blood, but the wound had completely healed.

"Drop the knife," Alcea said. It clattered to the floor. "Don't do that again. In fact, you are forbidden from committing suicide in any way, unless I give the command. Now *sit*."

He sat on the floor, shaking, and rubbed his wrist, which was sore despite being healed.

"What exactly did you expect to accomplish from that, anyway?" Alcea asked him.

"You know I'm mortal now. Killing Millicent won't change that."

"So you were trying to save her? You'd die, and she would be safe, and I'd be left with nothing? You honestly think I'd let it end there?"

She flitted to the wooden chair and sat, resting her Gremlin chin in one hand, thinking. Sebastian wanted to plead with her, but he knew it was useless. Once the beast had decided something, he was powerless to stop her.

"Still," Alcea said after a while, "now that you're mortal, there's no point in keeping you. I wonder… What memories did you show that magician, anyway?"

Eight

Spells and Secrets
Brought to Light

The news of that the Queen of Styx was in Chiaroscuro, and that she would not be surrendering any shadow goblins to the Empire, spread like wildfire. Several members of the Council—signified by their orange clothes—met Delilah and the humans as Misha led them inside in order to obtain some sort of dinner, and it was then that Delilah insisted they hold an official meeting—the next morning—and claimed ownership of the king's chambers, which Sebastian had, according to her, chivalrously insisted be given to the rightful ruler of the city, since he himself did not need sleep.

Thus Delilah, Dolly, Emmaline, and Millicent spent the night in Sebastian's old quarters, while Bostwick and Clarence roomed with Misha in the room where Millicent had been held (Millicent was embarrassed to learn that this was, in fact, Misha's own apartment; during her stay, he had been sleeping in the closet containing his memories). Despite everything that had happened that day, and in a large part because of it, everyone decided to postpone further discussion of what to do about Alcea and her true identity until the following morning before meeting with the Council.

"Maybe she wants to make an army of immortal beasts to take over the world," Clarence suggested over breakfast in the king's chambers.

"Then why let the students experiment on them?" Bostwick asked. "And why disappear after what happened to Inez?"

"I think she's after something on a smaller scale," Emmaline said. "When we met her in her cave, she was mostly concerned with treasure and sentimental items. She might just like Sebastian because he's a rarity, in terms of living creatures. Maybe we could trade her something else really rare in exchange for his contract."

"But how are we going to get to her cave?" Millicent asked. Despite everyone's reassurances, she was still concerned for Sebastian's safety now that he was mortal.

"In my letter," Dolly said, feeding Jill a piece of cabbage, "I asked Delilah's father to send us a new airship as soon as he builds one. It might take a while, but that will give us time to figure out how to deal with an immortal beast. Speaking of which," she said, grabbing several rolls and shoving them into her bindle, "I'm going to see if there might be any information in the library. You never know what document someone might have hidden away. Libraries are a bit like reposeums in that respect."

"Sure…" Emmaline said as Dolly left, taking Jill with her. "She's right about one thing though—we should use this time to plan. When we get to the Archipelago, Alcea will just make Sebastian attack us again. We need a strategy." Delilah raised her hand in the air, and Emmaline added, "One that doesn't involve killing him."

"Rude! I already promised Millie I'd let him live, although you know, Millie, the way things are going…"

"We're not killing anybody," Millicent stated matter-of-factly.

"Very well, then. I suggest we seal his magic with befuddlium."

"If we could get that close to him," Bostwick said.

"We could seal his magic some other way," Millicent suggested.

"No good," Delilah said. "The poor Domino is out for the count. We'll just have to knock him unconscious by repeated blows to the head."

"But even that might not do it," Emmaline said. "Who knows how the contract works? His body might act of its own accord when he's not awake."

"Well, I hate just sitting here doing nothing. In fact," the queen cried, leaping to her feet. "I've got to address my people, talk to the Council, and whatnot. Clarence and Emmaline, accompany me as ambassadors from the Empire! Bostwick, stand behind me and act cringingly servile."

"No," he said flatly.

"Actually," Millicent said, "I wanted to talk with Bostwick about some spells."

"Very well," said Delilah. "I leave him in your charge, Millie. Ta-ta, you two."

She took her small entourage and left Millicent and Bostwick alone. The only sound came from the patter of rain on the balcony and a distant roll of thunder.

"I think I have an idea about how to seal Sebastian's powers," Millicent began, "but, well…"

"What is it?"

"I was thinking about Alistair and the books I learned magic from, and I think maybe he might have changed over the years. Maybe he became a better person. All the spells I read seemed, you know, not so bad. What if the spell that makes shadows disappear wasn't intended to kill shadow goblins? What if it just seals their magic for a while?" Millicent had been considering the possibility all night, but wanted to hear Bostwick's opinion, as he had been formally educated in magic.

"That could be it," he said after a moment of consideration. "Have you ever cast that spell before?"

When she shook her head, he took one of the pitchers that had been brought up during breakfast and set it in front of her, where it cast a feeble shadow due to the light coming from the cloudy sky outside. Millicent placed her hands on the table where the pitcher's shadow fell. After a few seconds, the shadow faded away, but just as it disappeared completely, the pitcher itself vanished into nothingness, followed by the table itself.

"Oh no!" Millicent leaped back as the cups and bowls from breakfast fell to the ground and shattered.

"It's all right," Bostwick said as he repaired the dishes and stacked them in the corner of the room. "I'm not sure how to get the table back, though."

"I'm just no good at vanishing spells." She glanced sideways at her green hair.

"You'll get it eventually."

"But what if Alcea finds a way back to Chiaroscuro and makes Sebastian attack us again? Without the Domino, this is the only way to stop him without hurting him."

Bostwick sat back in his chair and muttered, "We might be able to refine the spell if we work the rest of the day."

"Couldn't you do it, Bostwick?"

"Me?"

"I could teach you the spell. I'm sure you'd know how to do it as soon as I explain. And you already know how to control your magic, so…"

"Well, it's worth a try."

He pulled a handkerchief out of his pocket and made it levitate so that it cast a rectangular shadow on the floor, then knelt down and waited for Millicent's instructions.

"Okay," she began, kneeling beside him and holding her hands up in front of her face. "Make your hands flat, with your thumbs out like this. And then put your thumbs and forefingers together so they make sort of this spade shape." Bostwick did so and placed his hands on the shadow. "Now you have to will the shadowy area to be flooded with light."

"Oh!" Bostwick said, vanishing the shadow in an instant, leaving the handkerchief unchanged. "It's not a vanishing spell at all. It's a summoning spell."

"What do you mean?"

"Well, a shadow is just a place without light, so what we're doing is conjuring light to fill the space. Which means that this spell couldn't possibly hurt Sebastian."

Millicent beamed at him.

"Um, anyway," he said, returning the handkerchief to his pocket, "you should practice it, too, just in case."

He conjured a rose and laid it on the floor for her to try the spell on; she vanished the shadow and most of the petals.

"Just focus only on the light," he said, conjuring another flower. "Don't try to make anything disappear."

By the fifth try, Millicent could do the spell perfectly.

"How long do you think the spell will last?" she said, gathering up the shadow-less bouquet.

"We'll just have to wait and see."

Millicent nodded and wondered how to pass the time. There wasn't anything more they could do to help Sebastian right now, but she felt guilty doing nothing while he was in Alcea's clutches. Of course, she reminded herself, Bostwick was technically Delilah's prisoner, and wouldn't be getting freed anytime soon either, unless…

"Um, while we wait," she said, "could we practice some more tricks? I know we don't have any hats, but I still have my deck of cards."

"All right. You already know how to levitate a few cards at once, so let's work with the whole deck."

Bostwick had her levitate more and more cards, until she could manage all fifty-two, then suggested they move onto other tricks. All the while, they kept an eye on the bouquet to see if the shadow had returned. So far, it had been almost two hours, and there had still been no change.

"Maybe it's permanent," Millicent said, glancing at the flowers as Bostwick finished explaining how to summon a specific card to the top of the deck. "I don't want to vanish Sebastian's shadow forever…"

"We can wait a little longer," Bostwick suggested, checking his watch again.

"Okay… I guess I'll try summoning the ace of clubs."

Bostwick nodded and shuffled the deck, then handed it to her.

"Unfortunately," he said, "I don't think any of the tricks I show you will help with Alcea."

"I know that," she said, donning a theatrically sly smile, "although I do have an ulterior motive in learning them. Weeks ago, Delilah promised me that as soon as you teach me every spell, you won't be bound to serve her anymore."

She pulled the top card, a three of spades, and frowned.

"She really said that, huh?" Bostwick asked, splitting the deck to reveal the ace of clubs. Millicent shuffled the cards again. "Still, there's no need to rush your magical training."

"But don't you want your freedom, Bostwick?"

"Sure, but whether Delilah acknowledges me as her butler or her court magician, she'll still treat me the same way. It honestly doesn't make that much of a difference anymore."

"Then you… don't want to go back to the Empire?"

"To tell the truth, Styx is sort of growing on me. I'm serious," he added when Millicent raised a skeptical eyebrow. "Having the country threatened every five minutes will still take some getting used to, but goblin food isn't so bad, and the citizens aren't half as crazy goblins in some of the other countries. I think I'd even miss Delilah if I left, though I'd never tell her that."

"Well, I guess if that's how you really feel…" Millicent said, smiling down at the cards in her hands.

"It is, but… Do you want to stay in the Empire after you graduate from the Academy? I assumed you'd want to live in Styx, but we don't have to stay if you don't want to—"

Bostwick clapped his hands over his mouth and turned beet red.

"I mean…" he mumbled, "not 'we', as in… I just meant… don't worry about me—or Styx—because you should focus on going to the Academy."

"Bostwick…"

He tried to look anywhere but at her as the blushing spread up to his hairline, then finally reached over and grabbed the bouquet, which once again had a shadow.

"One hour, fifty-three minutes," he said, becoming immersed in the face of his pocket watch. "I-it might be a little different on magical shadows. We can ask Misha to try it on his later, maybe."

"Um, Bostwick…" He seemed to freeze, not responding, so Millicent continued. "What if, well… what If I didn't go to the Academy?"

"But you've always wanted to."

"I did, but… since you and Sebastian started teaching me instead of Delilah—nothing against her, but she's not very good at explaining how magic works—a-anyway, I guess, well… going to the Academy doesn't really matter that much anymore. I like learning magic like this—with you."

"You really don't want to go?"

She shook her head.

"You're *one-hundred percent* sure?"

"I am," she said, relieved to get this confession off her chest, but shaking at the thought of what to say next. "So… you… you really wanna stay in Styx?"

"I want to stay with *you*," he said, "wherever that is."

He took her hand in his, and she leaned toward him.

"Brilliant!" they heard Delilah cry from the hallway.

They moved away from each other just as she marched into the room.

"Remind me to make Clarence a knight or something, Bostwick. He's simply brilliant."

"I thought you were talking to the Council," Millicent said, tucking a strand of hair behind her ear.

"I was indeed. The Council was of course happy to learn that I have declared them all citizens and unanimously voted to accept me as their queen, not that they had any choice in the matter. We decided not to mention everything about Sebastian all at once to them. It would be a bit of a shock to learn that their king had just been contracted into slavery and kidnapped. The official story is that I've 'talked things over with him' and he has agreed to give up his kingship. Needless to say, he won't be showing up for any official ceremonies any time soon."

"Why is it that when you explain it," Bostwick said, "it sounds like more of a coup than anything else."

"Oh, hush. The Chiaroscurans are ecstatic about having me as their queen. They actually used those exact words. And there are going to be balls and parties, and I'm going to get to make speeches. I don't think any goblins have ever been so excited about being associated with Styx." She blinked rapidly, wiped her eyes, and took a calming breath. "B-but I'm getting ahead of myself. Anyway, what have you two been up to?"

"Just practicing some spells," Millicent said, then looked down, blushing, "and talking."

Delilah grabbed Millicent's shoulders, then pointed one

hand accusingly at Bostwick. "What did you say to her, you rapscallion!"

"I didn't say anything."

"Her face is red, Bostwick! The telltale sign of Millicentian embarrassment, and you dare claim innocence?"

"He really didn't say anything," Millicent explained, "or, well…"

"Or? Well? 'Or well' he really did say something terribly horribly awful, but you're a lady, so you daren't repeat it? Is that what you're trying to say, Millie?"

"What exactly do you picture me talking about?" Bostwick asked, sounding vaguely affronted.

"Who can say, Bostwick? Clearly respectable company can't." She let go of Millicent and grabbed Bostwick by his lapels, wrenching him up from the floor. "Out with it, before I it without you! Wait, that doesn't make any sense."

"We just decided that… we'd like to stay together," Millicent said, before Delilah could think of an actual threat. "Even after I'm done learning magic and after Bostwick is free. That's all. R-really."

Delilah's eyebrows disappeared behind her bangs as she looked back and forth between the two humans.

"Am I to understand that you have finally confessed your love for one another?"

"I see you've given up on subtlety," Bostwick said. "What if we hadn't?"

"So that's a yes?"

"Basically."

Delilah shut her eyes, released Bostwick, shrugged her shoulders and said, "There's really no need to thank me."

"We didn't."

"No, really. This is your moment. I barely had anything to do with it. But, lest you be tempted, I'll say 'you're welcome' all the same."

"You're obnoxious, you know that?"

"Oh, Bostwick. You don't mean that. People say crazy things when they're in love."

"Really obnoxious," he said, though Millicent apparently found Delilah highly amusing, as she was stifling a laugh.

"Well, don't let me hold you back," Delilah said. "Go enjoy the sights of the city on your first romantic outing."

"That's really all right," Bostwick said, picking up the deck of cards. "We were already doing something, so—"

"Look," she said, laying a hand on his shoulder, then clasped her fingers down like a vice. "You can't just declare your love to a girl and then act like it never happened. That's what scoundrels do. You're no scoundrel, are you, Bostwick? No, I didn't think so. So you *will* take Millie out on a pleasant outing, you *will* buy her a delicious ice-cream cone or Chiaroscuran equivalent, and you *will* take part in a charming activity such as a hay ride, taffy-pull, or clam bake, or I *will* add a thousand years to your sentence and ruin your every waking moment, understand?"

"It's all right, Delilah," Millicent said. "I'd prefer to stay here and practice magic right now."

"Fine," the queen said as Bostwick wrenched his shoulder away from her, "but you're coming to the ball."

"What ball?"

"It'll be lovely, Millie. To celebrate Chiaroscuro becoming part of Styx, the shadow goblins are throwing a ball tonight.

It was Clarence's idea…"

"Sounds like it," Bostwick muttered.

"…to bring some levity after everything that's happened. Don't make that face, Bostwick. We're all guests of honor, so we're all going to attend."

"I think it sounds exciting," Millicent said. "I've never been to a ball before."

"They aren't all they're cracked up to be." Bostwick took a seat beside her once more. "It's just dancing, mostly."

"Tut tut." Delilah waved a finger in the air. "Human balls may be so, but goblins have more entertaining customs. There's generally a variety of exotic animals on display, all cooked and dead, of course, though not always in that order. There is of course conversation and dancing, but it generally turns into arguing and dueling, then into declarations of all-out war. Hmm… Come to think of it, I can't recall a single goblin military conflict that *didn't* start during a party."

"So, about that clam bake," Bostwick said, turning back to Millicent.

"Oh, hush," Delilah said. "We can't very well fight with our own countrymen. That just wouldn't be civil. Now, you can practice magic for now, but I'll be sending up servants with changes of clothes at some point. Can't have you looking like a scruffian with the rags you've got on, Bostwick."

"It's only because I've slept in them for two nights while I've been running around trying to save *your* country."

"Pshaw! People will think I couldn't afford to hire a proper butler and I had to pick one up off the street. Hmm… You really ought to be seen by a tailor, but we don't have time for that. I'll just send Misha to ask you for your measurements later. He's my new steward, you know? I seem to have picked up quite a few servants since inheriting Sebastian's kingship. But as for *you*, Millie, I was hoping to get a dress made for you specia—"

"That's ok! I think I still have a couple dresses in Misha's room from when I was here last."

"But I already thought of a design."

"It's fine," the humans said in unison.

"Very well," Delilah said, sweeping to the doorway. "I can tell you two want to be alone. I have official duties to attend to, after all, and I'm sure you have a lot to talk about. Hopes, dreams, plans." She swung around the doorframe out into the hall, then popped her head back in. "And don't forget: kobolds," she said, and was gone.

Nine

The Goblin Ball

By sunset Millicent and Misha were ready and waiting at the base of the southern staircase, where they had been told to stand before being let into the ball once the queen and her entourage were announced. The ball itself was being held on the bottom floor of the atrium; Millicent caught glimpses of the immense space beyond as shadow goblins pushing carts of food or carrying lanterns slipped in and out through the door. So far, none of the others had shown up. Misha had just gone to look for them when Emmaline and Dolly arrived.

"You aren't dressed up," Millicent said, noticing that Emmaline had on a simple blue tunic and pants.

"I barely had time to put my hair up. After settling everything with the Council, I went to the library and started reading through stacks of books. It turns out that the Chiaroscurans know a lot more about immortal beasts than you might think."

"I told you," Dolly said with a self-satisfied smile. "Let's see… I found a few references to one known immortal beast in Aphasia, one in Gammon, one in Catawampus—"

"That one's Shujaa," Emmaline said, "the map we met in the Catawampus Library. Apparently, sometime during the Bedlam War—that is, the war that decided the border between Catawampus and Gammon—Duplicity Jinx, the Catawampian general, managed to befriend Shujaa and turn the tide of the war. After the boundaries were agreed upon, Duplicity used Lessarian magic to seal the map of their country into his back."

"Lessarian?" Millicent asked. "You mean like Delilah's father?"

"Exactly. Duplicity's actions earned her people the right to govern what is now Lesse's Moor, despite being considered 'less-than-goblin, human-look-alikes' by the Catawampians. That's what the library book said, anyway."

"Hmm," Millicent said, slightly lost.

"Anyway, the whole reason I read about Shujaa was because of what Duplicity did to him. Lessarian goblins have the ability to infuse objects with magic; they call it mechano-magical invention. That's how Delilah's father created the airship."

Millicent nodded.

"Well, somehow Duplicity sealed magic into an immortal beast, turning his potential form into actuality. That prevented him from changing his form, so the borders of Catawampus would stay the same and there wouldn't be any more land disputes."

"So… we could have a Lesserian goblin seal Alcea's power?"

"Or at least lock her into one form. It would give us something to bargain with, or at least give us a chance if it comes down to fighting. And the best part is that there's a Lesserian goblin on our side who is hopefully building another airship and rushing here as we speak."

"Yeah!" Dolly said, throwing her fist into the air. "Hooray for libraries!"

"What are you all so excited about?" Bostwick said, coming up to them with a look like a man awaiting his own execution.

"Why are *you* so gloomy?" Emmaline asked.

"Aside from the prospect of whatever lies in store for us at a goblin ball, there're these clothes." He gestured to his attire, which consisted of the plain black tunic and pants that had been brought for him earlier that day.

"What's wrong with them?"

"They're exactly like my old uniform. I feel like I'm back at the Academy."

"Oh," Millicent said, "that's why I like them. I even made my underskirt yellow with a color changing spell. I thought it would make me look like a first-year student."

"And you're *sure* you don't want to go to the Academy?"

She nodded, grinning sheepishly. "I just like the aesthetic."

"Well, it looks good on you. Mine just make me feel so…"

"The word you are looking for," said Delilah, floating up to them with Clarence and Misha at her heels, "is 'underdressed'."

The queen herself wore an impeccably styled black-and-white asymmetrical dress with boots, gloves, and trousers to match. Clarence, likewise, had on a suit that must have been hand-tailored to his exact measurements.

"What was that about not having time for a tailor?" Bostwick asked.

"You were busy doing magic and reciting love poems, I'm sure. I, on the other hand, had all day to prepare."

"Shouldn't you have been talking to the Council?"

"Nonsense. I have servants for that."

Emmaline raised an eyebrow, then sighed and shook her head.

"Um, anyway," Misha said. "If everyone's ready, I'll announce you now."

He slipped through the door and for a moment they all held their breath, unable to hear what was being said on the other side, and then a chorus of music blared from within.

"That's our cue," Delilah said. "Be sure to smile. That means you, Bostwick. Millie, link arms with him. Now he can't claim to be unhappy. All right, here we go!"

They entered to music, cheers, and clapping, but what stole their attention was the lighting. There were rows and rows of glass bottles and jars hanging from wires stretching across the atrium, zigzagging up through ten stories. Each bottle glowed in a rainbow of colors caused by both the contents of the bottles and the tint of the glass.

"It's beautiful!" Millicent said, oblivious to the stares she and the other humans were receiving from the crowd of shadow goblins.

"It was Danika's idea," Misha explained.

"Heh," Danika said, peering at her work so that her pince-nez momentarily sparkled. "They all laughed at my fascination with light-making chemicals inside of a shadow.

Well, who's laughing now?"

"I think it's wonderful," Millicent said. "It reminds me of how colorful your memory bottles looked, Misha, against the white of everything else."

"Actually, those *are* my memory bottles. I figure I don't need to make fake memories anymore, since we can start making real ones out in the world."

"That's probably for the best, considering…" Bostwick said, then did a double-take at Danika. "What is that?"

Perched atop her head at a rakish angle was a minute green top hat.

"Eh? Oh, well, hmm. You see, I know it's technically illegal to possess your own hat, but it's a special occasion."

"But where did you get it?" Bostwick said, surveying the largely monochromatic crowd of goblins—dotted every so often with a red-clad guard. Here and there, he would spot a goblin wearing a crimson scarf or emerald gloves, and no small number were sporting hats of various sizes, colors and styles.

"You just have to know the right kind of people," Danika muttered as Bostwick pulled away from Millicent and fought his way through the crowd to Delilah, who had been swept away by admiring Chiaroscurans.

"Ah! Here he is now! My loyal butler!" she cried, then added in loud whisper, "He also does magic."

Half of the goblins "oohed" and the other half backed away nervously.

"Delilah, have you seen how many hats there are here?" he whispered.

"I had noticed. It seems formal attire in Chiaroscuro

involves bending the rules of occupational color and head dress a bit."

"Shouldn't we ask them to get rid of them?"

"And cause widespread panic?" she said with a wide smile, leading him through the crowd. "Though I love panic, I feel now is not the time. Come, now, I've told the Council all about you and they have prepared a dinner setting just for you."

"But what about Alcea?"

"She's probably fawning over Sebastian as we speak. It's not like Chiaroscuro will be any threat to his immortality if he's so far away. Magical love waves or whatever Emmaline was talking about don't reach that far, right? And even if she does show up, the party is crawling with palace guards. Now, as the Council's honored guest, you shall take the first bite, as is the Chiaroscuran custom…"

She sat him down at a long table already occupied by a number of goblins wearing fancy orange clothing, identifying them as council members. In front of him was a plate of unidentifiable, though mouthwatering, meat and vegetables. Pleased to find something at the ball that might actually be to his liking, Bostwick looked for something to eat with. On one side of the plate was a row of a dozen forks running off to the left. One the right side, it was the same. Knowing that he had to at least start on the outside and work his way in, Bostwick took his chances and reached for the outermost fork on the left, but was met with winces from the nearby shadow goblins. He tried for the outermost right instead, but the sharp intake of breath from the woman next to him told him that couldn't be it.

"You did this on purpose, didn't you," Bostwick said, grabbing the innermost left. An elderly goblin opened his eyes so wide that his monocle dropped into his drink.

"Whatever do you mean?" the queen said, purring as she leaned on the back of Bostwick's chair.

"It's not much of a ball, is it?" Clarence said, swirling his wineglass around in his hand. They had been gawked at by almost everyone in attendance and had finally had a few goblins bold enough to make conversation with them, but the evening had otherwise proved uneventful.

"I think it's fun," Millicent said, waving goodbye to a young goblin who had requested her and Clarence's autographs. "Even if it is a little awkward having everyone stare at us the whole time. Maybe you and Bostwick should do a magic show for them?"

"No, no, no. Balls are supposed to have dancing. If there's no dancing, it's not really a ball."

"You should probably tell that to the Council," a scruffy-looking goblin with an orange sash said. "They've never thrown a ball before. I suspect they did it to make you humans feel at home."

"Augustus!" Millicent said. "What are you doing here?"

"Heard there was free food," he said, tilting his head toward a buffet table that took up an entire wall. "Plus the Empress decided that she ought to make an appearance, seeing as it's her empire that's accepting our personhood and all that. I'm sure she's around here somewhere."

"Let's see if we can spot her," Clarence said, peering

through the crowd. "What markings does she have? Mostly black or mostly wh—What am seeing?"

Augustus and Millicent followed his gaze to a pillar near one of the exits where Emmaline and a buxom shadow goblin were seated. They had a piece of paper between them and were going over it intently.

"What in the world are you doing?" Clarence asked, striding over to them with Millicent in tow.

"Shh," Emmaline said without looking up. "Now, if you're used to brewing leaves from plants in the Wastes, then you might prefer herbal tea. I suggest rooibos or chamomile."

"Ooh!" her goblin companion said, "put me down for a case of each. My patrons would love to try teas from the Empire."

"If you want something really exotic, why not try 'true tea'?"

"You mean... camellia sinensis? I've only heard about that in stories!"

"I'll put you down for twenty cases. Five green, five black... Maybe some oolong?"

"You're selling tea?" Clarence asked incredulously.

"I'm doing my royal duty," Emmaline said.

"This is supposed to be a ball! You can't just lounge around making social connections!"

"That's what balls are for, Clarence. Mr. Charles makes most of his deals at parties like this. So," she said, turning back to the goblin, "we'll have to work out the currency exchange between the Empire, Styx, and Chiaroscuro with Delilah and the Council..."

"Something's got to be done about this," Clarence said.

"The situation is dire."

"Well," Millicent said, "at least they're playing a waltz. Maybe if you start dancing, the Chiaroscurans will follow suit."

"Not a bad idea. Millicent!" he said, extending his hand. "May I have the honor of this dance?"

"M-me?"

"Well, of course. It was your idea."

"But I don't know how waltz!"

"It's easy, I assure you."

Millicent panicked, certain that every eye in the room would be on her if she danced. She was one of the only humans there, after all. As she looked wildly around her for some means of escape, she noticed, in the shadows at the very edge of the room, a long white braid of hair and an embroidered coat.

"I… Um…"

"You can just move your feet in a square. And I'll lead, so—."

"Sorry, Clarence," she said. "It's just… I don't really feel like dancing at the moment."

"Are you all right? Anything I can do?"

"No, I… I need to check on something."

"Hmm, well, then… Emmaline!" She looked up from shaking hands with the goblin she'd just made a tea deal with. "Do you know how to waltz?"

"Of course."

"Then, may I have the honor of this dance?"

"I'd be delighted," she said, stowing the tea contract in her pocket.

♠ ♦ ♣ ♥ ♣ ♦ ♠

Millicent made her way to where she had seen the goblin. She reminded herself that it probably couldn't be Sebastian, that there was no reason for him to be back. At the same time, she wanted to know he was safe, and hoped, even though she knew it was foolish, that Alcea would release him from his contract once she found out he was mortal.

The edge of the atrium was covered by the overhang of the second floor and was separated from the main area by a row of columns. There were no lanterns strung up, and it was difficult to see, but Millicent could just make out the form of someone standing behind one of the columns.

"Sebastian?" Millicent said, still staying within the main body of the atrium.

"Not quite," said the goblin, coming to the edge of the shadows. She had a diamond marking over one eye.

"A-Alcea."

"I thought I might get your attention wearing this coat. Now listen. If you alert anyone to my presence, Sebastian is as good as dead. Now, you are going to quietly follow me outside, and we are going to make a bargain in exchange for Sebastian's freedom and Chiaroscuro's safety."

"What kind of bargain?" She backed up a step toward the light.

"Don't sound so suspicious," she said, deftly snatching a hat off the head of a passing goblin with her shadow. "You'll find out if you follow me outside. If you refuse, I'll order Sebastian to kill himself with his own shadow. He's mortal now, as I'm sure you're aware."

Millicent nodded, thinking it over. She desperately wanted to help Sebastian, but feared what Alcea would ask in exchange for his freedom.

"I'll follow you," Millicent said, glancing back at the atrium, then stepped into the shadows.

Alcea didn't say a word as they traveled down a hallway that led to an exit on the palace's southeast side, then up a walkway leading to the city's upper levels. Millicent could hear sounds of merrymaking from some of the windows they passed, but there were no other signs of life on the streets of Chiaroscuro. Alcea finally stopped on a moonlit rooftop that resembled a city square.

"I'm going to get Sebastian," Alcea said, handing the hat to Millicent. "You'll stay here. I just have to give him some instructions first; it won't take long."

"But I still don't know what I'm supposed to trade for—"

Alcea had gone through the hat without answering, leaving Millicent alone on the deserted rooftop.

A clock on the side of the palace struck once and Millicent jumped. She placed the hat on the ground and stepped back, listening as the clock continued to chime. With each ring, she could feel her heart beat faster. Finally, an eighth chime rang out, echoed across the square, and faded. Millicent counted the seconds, hoping that whatever Alcea asked for would be easy to obtain.

Black mist finally ushered out of the top hat, materializing as Alcea and Sebastian. The latter stood completely still with a look of misery on his face. Millicent took a step towards him, but Alcea shook her head.

"He's been instructed to stand still and silent, until after we're done here. Now for our bargain. I will release Sebastian and never come to Chiaroscuro again. In exchange, you will make a new immortal being for me—"

"What!"

"—using the same method as the students at the Academy—you even look the part. You'll use a shadow, just as they did, only that will be the end of it. I'll take the creature back to my cave, you can have Sebastian's contract, and we shall never have to speak to each other again."

"But… But I can't—"

"You can, if you want him back," she said, laying a hand on Sebastian's immobile shoulder. "He showed you his memories of the students creating the Ancient Shadows; use your love for him as a source. Because if you don't do this for me, I will kill him myself."

"But…" Millicent said, trying to think up some excuse. Suddenly, she realized that the rooftop was lacking a crucial element to the shadow spell. "But there isn't any statue."

"Not necessary." Alcea pointed to the shadow at her own feet.

"Your shadow?"

"It will work, I assure you. One only needs the privation of the image of a living thing. I might lose the ability to perform shadow magic, but that's no great sacrifice. Now, kneel down."

Millicent knelt, but ignored Alcea's further instructions to place her hands on her shadow.

"I… I'm sorry," Millicent said.

"You will be, if you don't follow through with our bargain."

"No, I mean… I think I finally understand why you're doing all this, and… I'm just sorry."

Alcea raised her chin up for a moment, staring down her nose at the magician.

"If you understand so much, then hurry. It's a simple spell."

Millicent shook her head, took a breath, and then quoted what she had read in one of her three magic books years ago. "Magic is the exertion of a magician's will over an object. It is through magic that we can dominate the world around us." Looking up, she said, "I don't want to exert my will over another person. I know that you're lonely, and you just want to be around somebody like you, but you can't control someone else's *life* with magic. It was wrong when the students did it, and it would be wrong now."

Alcea did not reply, but took Millicent's hands with her shadow and forced them to touch the ground.

"If you don't turn my shadow into an immortal being," Alcea said, "I'll use it to kill Sebastian. You've seen his memories; you know what that looks like. So you already control his life, magician. It doesn't matter how much you wish it were otherwise."

Millicent looked down at the ground, feeling helpless, then noticed the position of her hands. She moved them so her thumbs and forefingers were touching.

"Empty shadow, nothingness, a hole in the light in which we stand…" she began, without meaning it. Instead, she silently willed Alcea's shadow to become flooded with light. It was her only hope of saving Sebastian's life. "…listen with a mind which is absent, obey my will's command."

Millicent focused her whole mind on summoning light and felt as if the spell was working, but so far, Alcea's shadow remained unchanged.

"Take on shape and substance, like dew forms from a mist, like breath brought forth from a corpse. Defy your form; exist!" As she spoke these final words, she shut her eyes, willing every ounce of her magic into Alcea's shadow.

"What?" Alcea said flatly.

Millicent opened her eyes to see that nothing had changed, except that her own hair had turned light brown.

"It happens when I use too much magic," she said in a hollow voice, "even when my spell doesn't work. I told you I couldn't do it… I'm not even a first-year student."

Alcea seemed genuinely at a loss for what to do next.

"Unbelievable," she finally muttered to herself. "Centuries of planning and research, years of waiting, an opportunity of success finally presents itself… and it's all felled by human incompetence."

"Um, you… you still have Sebastian," Millicent said, standing. "I know he's not immortal but… you did sort of help create him, P-Professor Hollyhock."

Alcea flinched at the sound of her other name, then picked up the hat and dusted it off.

"It's not the same," she said, and sped through it, leaving Sebastian behind.

As soon as she was gone, Sebastian regained the ability to move; the first thing he did was destroy the hat. Millicent wanted to ask if he was all right, or tell him what her failed plan had been, or ask how Alcea had figured out that he was mortal, but she burst into tears before she could say anything.

"Millicent?" Sebastian asked, not knowing what had come over her.

"You're okay," she sobbed.

"Thanks to you. But I'm sure Hollyhock will be back."

He offered her his hand to help her up

"But you're mortal now," she said, taking it, then noticed that his wrist was covered in dried blood. "What happened!"

She jumped to her feet, looking his arm up and down for a wound.

"That's how she found out," Sebastian explained, "but she healed it."

"She cut you!" Millicent asked. Sebastian wouldn't meet her eye. "Oh…"

"I had to show her so she wouldn't go after you. She thought you were making me mortal."

Millicent nodded, wiping away her tears with the back of her hand. "Well, now that she knows, it looks like she doesn't want you anymore."

"That may be so, but I'm sure she's planning something else."

"Maybe," Millicent said, not entirely convinced that this was true. "Either way, we should let everyone know you're back. We should probably wait until after the ball, though."

"Ball?"

"To celebrate Chiaroscuro becoming part of Styx."

"Oh. Delilah did say something about that, didn't she?" He sounded offended.

"You know she saved the city, don't you? Well, I guess Emmaline and Heather did most of the work, but still. Delilah really cares about all of the shadow goblins."

Sebastian didn't appear too convinced, but followed Millicent back to the palace anyway. Millicent, for her part, felt as if a weight had been lifted off her chest. As far as she was concerned, her inability to perform the shadow vanishing spell had saved Sebastian's life, and she was certain that Alcea was so disgusted by her magical ineptitude that she would never bother asking her to cast any spell again. She had never been so happy to fail a magic trick.

"All right," she said as they arrived at the doorway that led to the atrium. "I'll tell everyone what happened once the party settles down, but for now you can head up—" She stopped, remembering Sebastian's bloodied wrist. "Actually, wait just a second."

She stuck her head into the room and looked for someone she could ask for help. Emmaline and Clarence were amongst a sea of dancing Chiaroscurans, while Delilah's pink hair could be seen clearly at the other side of the room. They were too far to get to in a hurry, but finally, she spied a familiar face near enough to talk to.

"Augustus!" she called, waving at him. "I need your help with something."

Augustus detached himself from the buffet and wandered over to her.

"You called?"

"I need a… a favor. It's for the king."

"The king? Well, I don't know what good I'll be to him, but seeing as I've been moving in high class circles lately," he said, scratching his stubble, "why not?"

♠ ♦ ♣ ♥ ♠ ♦ ♠

Bostwick picked up the third fork on the right, the last to choose from. Someone at the table coughed lightly.

"I've tried every single one," Bostwick said, unable even to muster up enough emotion to be annoyed. "This food is probably freezing by now. Just tell me which one it is."

"Should we tell him?" Delilah asked, and the councilmen nodded. "All right, all together now."

"You eat it with your hands!" they said in unison, then fell on the table laughing as Bostwick pushed his plate away.

"You really shouldn't be teaching them bad habits," he said.

"Oh, come now, Bostwick. It was all in good fun. Besides, there's an entire smorgasbord over there. I just had to introduce you to the Council before you buried yourself in a plate of food. They really wanted to meet you."

"It's true," a mustachioed councilman said. "Some of us were a bit nervous to hear that the queen had magicians for a maid and butler, but when she told us that you were already friends with King Sebastian, we knew we had nothing to worry about."

"You know," Delilah said, ignoring Bostwick's confused expression, "they all practiced magic together? Sebastian taught Millie how to do some spells, and it was her prompting that convinced me to look into your city's situation. Magicians and shadow goblins can work together now."

"I must confess," one of the councilwomen said, "I've always wanted to see the Academy. I know it was a very dark place for our people, but it's also the birthplace of the Ancient Shadows. I want to learn about what happened to Jurek and Inez, and understand our history better."

"We'll arrange it, though it may take a while to set everything up," Delilah said confidently, not mentioning that Inez had been killed or that the current Academy president knew nothing about the Ancient Shadows. "But I do believe that the dancing has started. It is a ball, after all. Shall we?"

The councilmen happily left their chairs to join Emmaline, Clarence, and the others.

"I feel we should declare this party a success," Delilah said, taking the seat beside Bostwick. "Though it's still early. There might be time to whip up some international incidents."

"Let's not." Bostwick prodded the food on his plate with one of the forks, then finally stabbed a piece of meat and ate it. "You know," he said after several more bites, "that was an interesting spin you put on how we know Sebastian."

"Well, he was friends with you, before stabbing you in the back like the traitorous weasel he is. Telling the Council anything more would have led to awkward questions."

"But even so… What do you plan on doing about Sebastian, anyway, assuming we can deal with Alcea?"

"Hmm. I could curse him back to being a cat. Back to the dungeon. Hmm… but then Millie might want to check up on him and feed him fish."

Bostwick didn't answer her, and went back to eating in silence. He half listened as Delilah continued on about the most suiting punishments for Sebastian's many crimes, then switched to discussing the various outfits of the Chiaroscurans.

Finishing his meal, Bostwick looked out across the crowd of goblins.

"Where did Millicent go, anyway? She didn't leave already, did she?"

"Who are you to talk, Bostwick? I thought you said balls were boring."

"Well, maybe I wanna dance with her."

"Then we must find her!" Delilah squealed and floated several feet to see over the heads of the Chiaroscurans. "Hmm, I don't see her tell-tale hair anywhere. Still, we can't have you skulking here on the sidelines…"

"I'm not going to dance with you, just so we're clear."

"Don't be presumptuous, Bostwick. Besides, you're much too short. Ah! There she is, hiding by the buffet."

"Her hair's brown," Bostwick said, peering across the room. "Why would she—?"

"Irrelevant!" She landed and shoved Bostwick out of his chair. "It's not every day you get the opportunity to dance with the girl of your dreams, you know? Don't just sit there questioning her hairstyle!"

Bostwick maneuvered his way around the waltzing goblins—as much to escape Delilah as to get to Millicent—and found her on the other side of the atrium leaning her head out the door.

"Oh, hello, Bostwick! Um… one of the shadow goblins had to ask me about something."

"Are you all right? You look a little—"

"I'm fine," she said quickly. "I'm just… excited about everything."

"But what about your hair?"

"My hair? Oh!" She changed it back to green, then grinned. Bostwick stared steadily back. Her smile faltered.

"Well, I have something really exciting to tell everyone, but I want to wait until the ball's over. Right now, everyone should be enjoying themselves!"

"In that case," he said, holding out his hand to her, "would you like to dance?"

Panic filled her eyes, but she said, "I-I'd love to dance."

"You… don't have to if you don't want to. It's okay."

"But I *do* want to. It's just, I've never waltzed before and I don't want anyone to see me."

"If it helps, I don't think the shadow goblins really know how to waltz either. They seem to be making it up as they go along."

"And you won't mind if I mess up?"

"Of course not. I'm no waltzing enthusiast myself; it's just that it's not every day you get to dance… at a goblin ball."

"I guess that's true."

She laid her hand on his shoulder, and he placed his on her waist, talking her through the first few steps. After a few minutes of him leading, she seemed more comfortable, at least enough to look at him instead of her feet.

"It's not so bad, right?" he asked.

She nodded, but glanced quickly left and right.

"No one's watching us, "he assured her."

"R-right." She tilted her head toward the floor once more, but looked up at him with her eyes.

No one was watching them, Bostwick realized, and after making one last check that Delilah was nowhere in the vicinity, he leaned his head toward Millicent and kissed her.

It made dancing a little harder, but neither of them cared.

Ten

The Queen and King
of Chiaroscuro

"YOU DID WHAT?" Delilah shrieked.

"Shh," Millicent said, glancing at the shadow goblins that were still cleaning the atrium. It was past midnight and the ball had only just finished. Most of the Chiaroscurans had left, but Heidi and a dozen others were sweeping up the floor and removing dirty dishes. "It's okay. Alcea left on her own."

"You could have been killed, Millie!" She grabbed Millicent by the shoulders, then shook her back and forth on each word. "You. Could. Have. Died!"

"Well, I didn't," she said, taking a step back to steady herself.

"But is Sebastian all right?" Misha asked.

"Mostly. Augustus is watching over him in my… in Misha's room."

"That certainly inspires confidence!" the queen cried.

"Why didn't you tell someone where you were going?" Bostwick asked, clearly disconcerted by the fact that none of them had even noticed she had gone.

"There wasn't any time. She swept me out of the palace before I could even think about it."

"And then she just left, eh?" Delilah said, pacing back and forth. "I suppose a mortal Sebastian is rather useless, as far as possessions go, but still, she could have used him as a footstool or something."

"It's certainly suspicious," Emmaline said, "but for now, at least, we know that Sebastian's safe. We might as well talk to him and get any information he has on Alcea."

They made their way to Misha's apartment, bringing several large memory bottles for lighting. Rather than go inside, however, Delilah halted before the closed door.

"You must stay outside, Bostwick. You're liable to fly off the handle as soon as you see Sebastian and attack him for everything he put you through."

"Seriously? I think we have more to worry about right now than what happened in the past."

"Trust me. As your dear employer, I know you far better than you know yourself. Plus, it's an order."

Bostwick sighed and leaned against the wall while his companions entered the room to find Sebastian seated in the armchair. Delilah marched over to him, balled up her fist, and struck him across the jaw.

"That's for everything you've put us through!" she cried, as Augustus tried to restrain her and Misha looked on in confused horror, unsure which of the two monarchs he owed more allegiance to. Delilah shook free of Augustus and took a breath, then stared down her nose at Sebastian, who was rubbing his face. "You're lucky that's all you get. I would execute you right here on the spot except that a dead king would be hard to explain to the Council. But honestly, do you have any idea what you've done? Countries torn apart and scattered across the world? A bomb about to blow apart a city? And then putting Millie in danger when she went to go save you! I'd turn you into a cat right now if *someone* hadn't cut my Domino to pieces!"

She finished in a snarl and threw herself onto the sofa opposite Sebastian. Throughout this screed, he had said nothing and, far from staring defiantly back at her as he usually did, dropped his eyes to the floor.

"Well, what now?" Delilah asked, looking up at Millicent.

"Um, I'm pretty sure that Alcea isn't coming back for him, so——."

"I'm sure of just the opposite," Sebastian said. "Even if she doesn't want me as an immortal beast, I can still act as her slave. I can't feel her presence right now, but I'm sure Hollyhock will be back. She's not the sort of person to give up her... property so easily. If she's made up her mind, there's nothing you can do to stop her."

"True," Delilah said. "You're too dangerous to leave lying around. Emmaline, go find a guard and ask them to bring us some befuddlium. Then, at least, you won't be able to do too much damage."

"In the meantime," Millicent said after Emmaline left, "I thought we could have Bostwick seal his powers. He never had any trouble with that spell."

"Oh, very well. Come in, Bostwick, but try to restrain yourself!"

He turned around the door frame, but stopped a few paces inside, staring at Sebastian with an expression across between contempt and confusion. He continued walking, finally kneeling down to Sebastian's faint shadow cast by the glowing jars. He placed his hands on it, but nothing changed.

"That's strange," he said, standing. "It feels like something was about to happen, but I just didn't have enough power."

"That's how I felt," Millicent said. "Maybe it doesn't work on magical shadows."

"That's the spell you were trying to use?" Sebastian asked. "The one Alistair wrote… to use on me?"

"If you're talking about your plan to kill yourself, it it's the wrong kind of spell entirely," Bostwick said flatly. "I could have told you that a long time ago."

"What do mean? If it makes shadows disappear…"

Millicent shook her head. "It doesn't exactly work like that, or well, I guess it sort of does, but it wouldn't hurt you."

Sebastian stared at the floor for a moment, then slammed his fist against the arm of the chair.

"Then I dragged you into this for nothing!"

"Sorry we disappointed you," Bostwick snapped, scowling, and walked back to the door. "I'll be out here if any of you need me."

No one else could find anything to say until Emmaline returned, bringing Cecil with her.

"Your Majesty," the guard said to Sebastain with a salute, "this human says you are in need of some befuddlium in a hurry. In lieu of going down to the armory and getting some, may I offer mine?"

"The quicker my magic is sealed, the better."

"Yes, sir."

He withdrew a key from his pocket and unlocked his beffudlium collar and belt and traded them with Sebastian.

"Honor hereby restored," Delilah said. "There may be a promotion in your future. But how ever did you get a key?"

"All guards receive a master key to beffudlium restraints when we're instated. I've had it with me since my first day on the job."

"Even in prison?"

Cecil nodded.

"Ah, then in that case, honor hereby retracted," Delilah said. "Anyway, Sir Paws-alot, you better hide that befuddlium under your clothes when you're out and about. Now, since the royal chambers have been assigned to their proper owner, I suppose you shall stay in these quarters, but Misha and Bostwick will be so busy attending my every whim that we shall have to have someone else keep an eye on you. Cecil? No, that could end badly… Cecil *and* Augustus, since you are—I can't believe I'm saying this—the most informed goblins in the city, I want you both to act as… hmm…"

"Personal body guards to the king?" Cecil asked, eyes shining with unbridled excitement.

"Sure. Make sure one of you is with him at all times, and report to me if you notice anything suspicious, from him or anyone else."

Sebastian tugged on his collar experimentally, then said, "Now that there's no danger of me attacking anyone, I want to talk to you, alone."

"Very well," Delilah said, waving for everyone to leave the room. Only Cecil protested.

"But Your Majesties, you just said—"

"I can certainly handle myself against him. Now away with you."

Cecil followed everyone else into the hallway, but kept scanning their surrounding as if Alcea might leap out of nowhere at any moment.

Emmaline and Millicent, meanwhile, went to talk with Bostwick, who was leaning on the rail overlooking the atrium, where the memory bottles still emitted a faint glow. He and Emmaline sighed in unison.

"Don't look so worried," Millicent said. "If Alcea had really wanted him, she would have taken him with her."

"There probably isn't any use in trying to understand her," Emmaline said. "It's just that, if I wanted something so badly that I was willing to kill for it, I wouldn't just give up because you couldn't do the spell right away, and I certainly wouldn't give over my hostage."

"Maybe she didn't want to kill him after all, like she was bluffing."

"But she clearly has no respect for life—convincing Danika to bomb a city, sending Sebastian after you," she said, nodding at Misha, who joined them. "Why would she suddenly feel any differently about Sebastian? If she actually cared about him, he would have started to show mortal tendencies a long time before we met him. That's what I find so confusing about her: she wants to create an immortal being like her but if she ever ended up actually loving that person, they would turn mortal. Would she just stop loving them? Is she really so selfish that she just wants to own someone for the sake of it? That's just… awful."

"Yeah."

They stood for a moment, turning over the situations in their heads. Finally, Emmaline said, "What about you, Bostwick? You're looking more gloomy than ever."

"I was just thinking about what Delilah said, about Sebastian and me. Finally talking to him up close for the first time since I gave him the Domino, and listening to how disappointed he was that we couldn't kill him with magic... I did want to hit him."

"Please don't," Misha muttered.

"Don't feel bad, Bostwick," Millicent said. "I feel the same way."

He raised an eyebrow, and Emmaline actually laughed.

"Ok... maybe not exactly the same, but... to hear him say that he dragged us into his life for nothing made me really angry. I know he made friends with us just to get the Domino, and taught me magic so I could kill him someday, but... well..."

"Despite his horrible motivations, we still became his friends?" Bostwick said, looking no less miserable than a moment ago.

"Exactly."

"And even if his plans were all based on stupid assumptions, both about that shadow spell and about us, it doesn't change that fact?"

"See, Bostwick, I do feel the same way."

"Yeah. You're just as crazy as I am."

"You two should tell him how you feel," Misha said. "Show him that it wasn't all for nothing."

"Yeah!" Millicent cried. "Even if his suicidal plan didn't turn out the way he expected, that doesn't make it a failure!"

"Or something like that," Bostwick said, smiling despite himself.

Once Sebastian and Delilah were alone, he glanced sideways at her, saying, "Millicent said you were the one who saved Chiaroscuro from Hollyhock's bomb. Is that true?"

"The city's still standing, is it not?"

"Why?"

"Why?" she asked, sprawling sideways across the sofa. "What was I supposed to do, let everybody die?"

"I mean, why did you care?"

"What a terrible question! It wasn't a matter of caring or not. The Chiaroscurans are my people. The fact that I've grown rather fond of them in the past few days and would go to war with the entire Empire if they so much as look the wrong way at any of the shadow goblins doesn't matter. Even not knowing them, I had to save them. I think I would have done so even if they weren't citizens of Styx."

"Then you are claiming Chiaroscuro as your own?"

"It's in Styx already, isn't it?" She stood and walked in a small circle around Sebastian, then grabbed his braid and yanked on it. "You thought I'd leave them to be blown up, didn't you?"

He pulled his hair away from her over his shoulder without answering.

"A completely misguided assumption. I mean, it's not as if *I'm* the one running around destroying other people's countries." She floated around to see his expression, but he turned away from her and bit his index finger. "Hmm, nothing to say? Maybe you thought that after Chiaroscuro blew up, I would drop pieces of it in Catawampus and Gammon and Pandemonium? Maybe you thought—"

"I'm sorry," he whispered.

"Hmm?"

"I understand how you felt… when I asked you to destroy the map of Styx. It was the same way I felt when I found out what Hollyhock had planned for my people. I'm sorry I put Styx in danger." Delilah floated back down and started circling him again. Sebastian was aware of a slight purr emanating from her.

"But I won't apologize for thinking you would do something even worse to Chiaroscuro," he said. "Given everything I've heard about your family, and all the time I spent with you, there was no reason to suspect otherwise. But now… I think you will protect Chiaroscuro."

"Quite."

"And you'll need my help."

"Not quite. I've already handled everything while you were gallivanting around with Alcea and I don't see what help you could be now."

"I'll explain what's happening to the Council. They already know and trust me, and I'm sure once they understand the situation, they'll make sure all the hats in the city are destroyed. I can also describe Hollyhock to them and have the guards be on the lookout for her."

"Hmm, I suppose that might be useful."

"There's one thing I ask in return, which will hopefully end Hollyhock's interest in Chiaroscuro entirely." Sebastian closed his eyes, steeling himself. "I want you to kill me."

"Excuse me?" Delilah asked.

"I'm the only reason Hollyhock cares about the city, so I'm the one putting it in danger. And tonight, the reason Millicent tried to make a deal with her was to save me. If Hollyhock had hurt her, I don't know what I would have done."

Delilah sighed, shook her head, and cried, "Do you ask every woman you meet to kill you? You're a bounder *and* a cad!"

"You know I deserve it after everything I've done."

"Hmm… you really do. And it is up to me to execute you, since you're a Styxian citizen."

Sebastian felt slightly sick at the idea of being numbered as a Styx goblin, but he knew that this might be his only way of making up for his crimes, since Alcea had forbidden him from killing himself.

"In that case," the queen said at last, "on your end, you must not only talk to the Chiaroscurans about Alcea, but also encourage them to trust and love me. I'll be the one protecting them once you're gone, after all."

"I suppose…"

"Therefore, whenever there are Chiaroscurans present, you must treat me with the utmost respect, act friendly toward me, and refer to me as… Hmm, 'Your Majesty' is so impersonal. How about, 'my darling queen'?"

"I would rather die."

"You're going to anyway. I don't have to make it quick and painless."

"I'll call you 'Your Majesty', but nothing else."

"Lovely!"

"But you can't tell anyone about our agreement."

"I am the very model of secrecy. I won't breath a word of it. Now, it's getting late and I've agreed to meet with the Council tomorrow for breakfast. We can all eat together like one big family—plus the cat!"

She walked to the door laughing.

"Delilah," Sebastian called after her. "Before you... I want a chance to say goodbye to everyone."

"Don't be so dramatic," she said, flinging the door open. "Just worry about getting a proper night's sleep and dealing with tomorrow's problems when they come."

Eleven

Diplomacy and Double-Cross

"All this time," Bostwick said, looking across the room to where the heads of the Council were finishing their breakfast with Clarence, Sebastian, and Delilah, "and I never realized that Delilah was going easy on me."

Even from afar, the look of anguish on Sebastian's face was unmistakable. Delilah had already made a show of being led into the room on his arm, and was now gesticulating wildly as she spoke, every so often adding a pat to his head.

"She's telling them about their 'childhood friendship'," Emmaline said, joining Bostwick, Millicent, and Misha at their own table, "and how she rescued him from the dungeons of Styx."

"Poor Sebastian," Millicent said. "He hasn't eaten a single bite."

"I don't think he likes eating in front of people," said Misha. "He always waited for me to leave before eating whenever I brought him food and looked really annoyed if I came back before he was finished. I guess he never really had to eat before, so he doesn't know if he's doing it right or not."

"So there really is such a complex," Bostwick mused.

"But that's not good!" Millicent balled up her napkin and stood up. "I don't think he had anything for dinner last night, and now no breakfast?"

"We can sneak him some later—" Emmaline began, but Millicent had already crossed to Sebastian's table. After a brief conversation, the two of them left the room. Emmaline turned to her companions, both of whom had finished their meals. "You might as well go with her. I'm going to stay here in case Delilah does something…"

"Undiplomatic?" Bostwick asked.

"I was just going to say 'crazy'. Anyway, it might be a good time to talk to him about, you know…"

"Yeah," Bostwick said, grimacing at the prospect of finally confronting him. He had been spared from doing so last night by Cecil's exuberance at being able to have a private conversation with the king, which kept Sebastian occupied long after the rest of them had fallen asleep, but he couldn't put it off forever.

They found Millicent and Sebastian on a bench just down the hall, guarded at a distance by Augustus. Sebastian was chewing on a roll that Millicent had smuggled out, but sure enough, he pulled it away from his face and held his hand in front of his mouth as soon as they approached.

"So… did you explain to the Council what's going on?" Bostwick asked.

Sebastian nodded, swallowing. "They've already told the Captain of the Guard to have his men destroy all the hats in the city, properly this time, and explain the danger to everyone. Right now, Hollyhock's too far away for the contract to be in effect, since magic is limited by distance, but when she enters the city, I'll at least know what direction she's in. We can warn everyone to stay inside, away from her."

"And how are we supposed to fight her?" Augustus asked, coming closer. He had clearly been eavesdropping.

"We won't," Sebastian said. "Since Millicent can't do the spell she wants, the only reason she would have for coming back here is to retrieve me. Before that happens, I intend to have already… left the city, but should it come to it, I'll surrender myself to her." Millicent made a disappointed noise, so he said, "You know we can't go against her. Even if I am wearing beffudlium, she can still order to me to come with her or attack you physically if you try to stop me." He felt the chain mail belt under his shirt; Cecil had earlier removed the collar, which would have been too difficult to hide. "I knew the risks of making a contract with Hollyhock from the beginning, long before I met you. She's someone I have to deal with alone."

"Why can't you ever rely on anyone else?" Bostwick said.

"What?"

"Look, if you'd really wanted to find someone with the power to save Chiaroscuro, Delilah and her Domino would've been the safest bet, but you didn't even think of asking her for help."

"Delilah's the last person who would help me. Even now, I'm fairly sure she's only interested in becoming Queen of Chiaroscuro in order to bolster her own ego."

"That's probably partly true," Bostwick conceded, but was too annoyed with Sebastian's attitude to let the matter rest at that. "She also cares about its people, though. She was literally willing to cross the globe for the sake of her country, and she somehow managed to do it without betraying anyone." He crossed his arms and sighed. "I trusted you back in Styx, remember? And you used that trust to kidnap Millicent, just so she could relieve you of your guilty conscience by killing you. You've been using everyone for your own gains this whole time, and now you're acting like some sort of hero who has to face everything on your own?"

Sebastian bit his finger, unable to argue with any of it.

"If you'd just told us what was happening to Chiaroscuro when we first met," Bostwick continued, "we would have helped you. And now that Chiaroscuro is safe, you're our next priority."

"Exactly!" Millicent said. "You're our friend, Sebastian. We could never just give you up to Alcea. And we really do understand the risk we're taking."

Sebastian looked at each of them, a slight blue tinge to his cheeks. It was hard to tell if he was angry, pleased, or embarrassed, but Bostwick thought, after all his grandiose speeches, it was nice to see him actually thinking about what someone else said for once.

"Well it…" Sebastian began after some time. "It's probably a moot point, anyway."

"I agree," Millicent said. "There's no reason for her to come back now."

"Indeed," he said, not meeting her eye.

Bostwick and Millicent left him to eat in peace. They spent the rest of the day exploring the city, learning much about the Chiaroscuran way of life. It turned out that about half of the shadow goblins, regardless of occupation, did in fact live in the palace, which had been built with many family-sized apartments. Misha met up with them around lunchtime and gave them a tour of the outer and lower levels of city, which were grimier and more dilapidated than the lacy, white Empyreal Palace.

By nightfall, they arrived back at the Council Chamber, where Clarence entertained the councilmen with magic tricks, Emmaline pored over a number of documents, and Sebastian sat alone at the end of a bench, his two bodyguards forming something of a buffer between himself and Delilah. When the queen saw the two humans, she floated over to them. After a brief interrogation, she declared their day "a romantic outing of roaring success—so far", then demanded they eat alone up in the king's chambers, where she had prepared a surprise.

Though Bostwick made many a comment about what horrors awaited them, it turned out to be a normal meal—though everything was cut into the shape of a heart—lit by two magenta memory bottles. Millicent said it was cute, even if it did remind her a little too much of the pink dress incident, and they settled in to what was in fact a very pleasant—even *romantic*—evening, though Bostwick insisted they not admit as much to Delilah.

After dinner, he kissed Millicent goodnight and headed back down the staircase to the main part of the palace, casting a small flame spell. The few Chiaroscurans he saw seemed to find their way without the need of any light, and even recognized him enough to wave shyly or whisper about "the queen's magician" to each other as they passed by him.

One, a female goblin with a high ponytail and round glasses, nodded at him from an open doorway.

"There you are, Bostwick."

"Uh, hi," he said, trying to figure out how she knew his name. "Did we… meet at the ball?"

"Oh, we've never met, but I could never forget that face."

Suddenly, he felt his feet lift off the ground as his body rose into the air—something he hadn't experienced since levitation practice at the Academy—and found himself swept into the room with the woman, whose white hair turned black and whose skin lost its bluish hue as she let the illusion fade. He was face-to-face with a magician: Professor Hollyhock.

Though he still had his flame spell burning in one hand, he didn't think it would do much good against an immortal beast, and the only other way out of what broom closet they were in was a miniscule window leading to a twenty-story drop. Even calling for help might prove useless—or fatal—so he decided to play along for the time being.

"Alcea?"

"That's right."

"What do you want?"

"Right to the point. Excellent. I suppose Millicent told you about the deal I offered to her, and how she was unable to carry out her end of it?"

Bostwick was more than a little disturbed by the way she legalistically described giving Millicent a life or death ultimatum, but nodded.

"I'm offering you something similar. I'm sure that a magician as accomplished as you will be able to pull off the spell without a problem." He squinted at her suspiciously, so she lowered him to the ground and turned into a tall, scaly goblin and leaned on the door.

"Perhaps I should explain. I used the memory of that clingy little maid to see if I couldn't find some way of helping her to realize her magical abilities. Though it was almost a complete waste of time—I honestly feel swindled, being convinced to trade for such a thing—I did remember something worthwhile: how awed she was of *you*, the first in your class at the Academy, a prodigy."

"So you want me to do what Millicent couldn't. But we already have Sebastian, so…"

"You don't have his contract, but that's irrelevant for *our* bargain. I was planning on trading you something else."

Bostwick felt like someone had punched him in the stomach. He could already tell whose life would be used for a bargaining chip this time, but waited for Alcea to say it out loud.

"Name your price," she said.

"What?"

"Don't be obtuse. I can tell that you're no bleeding heart—it was you who traded an entire country to escape from the Queen of Styx, remember? And if that girl's memory can be believed, cutting through her girlish admiration, you're a sensible, straightforward person who says what needs to be said and does what needs to be done. As for myself, I don't *like* strong-arming people when I can trade with them instead, and I seem to have finally found someone willing to listen to reason instead of threats. So… what is it you want? Power? Money? Perhaps to finally be free of that goblin queen? You hate it in Styx; I remember. Surely there's something that's worth the price of one little spell."

A spell, Bostwick thought, that equaled a goblin's life in what would probably end up being eternal servitude. He felt slightly insulted by her bleak opinion about his motivations, but it meant that Millicent was safe for now, and her offer, as baffling as it was, might be their only chance at dealing with her once and for all.

"I want…"

"Yes?" she asked, turning into the professor once more.

"I want… to sign a contract."

"Oh?"

"I *am* sensible, and I know you've used loopholes in the past to manipulate the circumstances of bargains. That's not going to happen this time. I'm not trading anything with you until I sign a contract and agree to every word on it… and I want Emmaline to write it. She's the only one I'll trust to make it airtight."

"You really are more agreeable than that other magician! Very well, decide on your terms and talk with this Emmaline person. I'll give you until tomorrow morning at nine o'clock. There should be a good shadow cast at that time."

"Where will we meet?" He didn't bother to ask what would happen if he didn't show up.

"I don't want us to be disturbed. There is a hat out in the Wastes, close to the seashore. Have Misha bring you. He won't remember anything, one way or another. And I'm sure it goes without saying that, aside from him, you need to come alone."

"I understand… I can really ask for anything?"

"Anything."

She disappeared for a moment, or so Bostwick thought, until he noticed a tiny beetle fly out the window. Bostwick waited a full minute after she left, then ripped open the door and headed to the Council Chamber.

"I've been meaning to ask you," Augustus said, walking with Sebastian to Misha's room, "with all this talk with the Council, are we allowed to go to the Empire now, or are our lives forfeit as soon as we cross Styx's border?"

"I'm sure the queen would go to war if they tried to dissect any of us," Cecil said.

Sebastian nodded. "I'll trust Emmaline to arrange things with the empress. The old empress made it illegal to perform such experiments, but considering how much the average magician knows about the Ancient Shadows, they might not know such a law exists."

When they came to their room, they were set upon by a scrawny goblin wearing a purple scarf, who actually leapt off the floor and onto Augustus. Luckily, she was too light to knock him over.

"Augustus!" she cried with a determined pout. "You left me at the party. I got lost and had to haunt the hallways."

"Lost? You said you lived in the palace."

"I lived in the *Imperial* Palace, not the *Empyreal* Palace."

"Now I'm lost."

"There's no need to worry, miss," Cecil said. "As a member of the Chiaroscuran Order of Law, you can depend on me to help you find your way home."

The Empress shook her head and coiled her arm tightly around Augustus, refusing to let go of him as Cecil tried to pry her away

Not wishing to add any fuel to this strange situation, Sebastian walked past them into the room. Though all he had done that day was talk with people, he felt more exhausted than ever before and attributed it all to Delilah's presence. Now that he was finally alone—the only sounds being the argument on the other side of the closed door and the slight buzz of an insect—he felt he could finally relax and unbuttoned his tunic.

"That explains it," said a voice from the insect, which in an instant turned into a wyrm. She shoved Sebastian to the floor and ripped the befuddlium restraints off with her claws, then tossed them away from him.

"Don't make a sound," she commanded, as he reflexively slashed through her with his shadow, "and don't move."

She took on her shadow goblin form, unaffected by being cut through with a shadow, and told Sebastian to stand up. "I was wondering why I couldn't feel where you were. That metal is really something else, blocking the power of the contract." She turned into a bloodhound to inspect the green belt before resuming her goblin form. "Hmm, it's imbued with phantasmal jellyfish ectoplasm and… whatever it is that causes this green color. Fascinating! Anyway… Do not touch any beffudlium, and let no one put any beffudlium on you. Don't tell anyone that I was here, and if anyone asks, say that you are still wearing those restraints. Button up your tunic. Do not leave this room until I tell you to. Do not warn anyone of any coming danger. You can speak now."

Without anything further, she turned into an eagle, clutched the beffudlium in her talons, and flew out the window. Any peace that Sebastian felt a moment ago was gone. He was now only aware of a vague sense of dread; Alcea was going to have him use his shadow on someone, at some point soon.

He finished buttoning his tunic and tried to step into the hall, but could not even cross the threshold. Though he had left them on the brink of an argument, his would-be guards and the other goblin were now laughing like old friends. It was if they occupied a completely different universe from the one he found himself in.

"So the Candlestick Maker has me in a headlock, through the bars," Augusts was saying, "and the Empress flounces over and pokes him right in the eye."

"You should join the Order of Law!" Cecil said. "We need that kind of exuberance on the force."

"Um," Sebastian said. They all turned to him in surprise, despite the fact that two of them were supposed to be keeping a constant eye on him. "I need your help. One of you needs to—" As soon as he tried to say "warn the humans", the contract rendered him mute. Even if he couldn't tell anyone about what had happened, he refused to sit around waiting to be used as a weapon.

"One of you needs to get Delilah for me as soon as possible. See that she comes alone."

"Yes, sir!" Cecil said with a salute, and ran off to do as requested.

Sebastian watched him head toward the stairs with a mix of apprehension and anticipation. He'd been waiting for this a long time, but even so, he didn't feel entirely prepared for it. Still, aside from atoning for his crimes, he had to escape Alcea before it was too late. Execution was the only way out that she hadn't thought of.

Twelve

Noblesse Oblige

Bostwick found Delilah and Emmaline on their way up to the royal chambers, discussing whether glowing upside-down flowers, gas lamps, or whatever type of automatic lighting they used in Catawampus would be best for Chiaroscuro, if they even needed such a thing. As soon as they saw Bostwick they hushed, as something was clearly wrong.

"Alcea showed up," he began, and told them of the entire conversation. There was no point in being subtle at a time like this.

"Shouldn't we tell the guards to be on a lookout for her?" Emmaline asked as Delilah started upstairs again.

"And what good would they be?" Delilah asked without turning around. "She can use shadow magic, and magician's powers, and transform into just about anything else. She sounds almost as powerful as the Domino of Nonpareil."

"Well, you technically defeated Sebastian when he was wearing that, so…"

"Precisely. We're the only ones who can handle this. I'm not going to throw random Chiaroscurans at her without having some sort of scheme."

Both impressed and disturbed by an actual show of forethought from Delilah, they followed her to the king's chambers.

"You didn't actually sign a contract, did you?" Millicent asked once they had filled her in.

"No. I was just buying time, but we don't have much, if I'm really going to meet with her tomorrow. I thought we could figure something out before then."

"Our best option," Emmaline said, "would be sealing her into a single form, using Lesserian magic, but we still haven't heard anything from your father yet, so…"

"Hmm…" Delilah paced around the room, obviously anxious, but still spoke in her usual smooth tone. "Suppose for a moment we did have a Lesserian here, Emmaline. What would he seal into her?"

"What do you mean?"

"Lesserian mechanomagical invention works by pulling magic from one thing—like a magical crystal or a will-o-wisp or whatever—and stuffing it into something else. So what magic would our hypothetical Lesserian stuff into Alcea?"

"I guess it could be anything. From what I read, it sounded like the magic itself is what turns an immortal beast's shifting, potential form into one specific, actual form. The magic doesn't have to be anything particularly special."

"Hmm… do you agree, Bostwick? Millicent?"

"You're asking me?" Millicent said.

"Well, of course. You studied from philosophically minded magic books that were all about forms and potentiality and being and essence. And Bostwick here was a moderately good student, I've heard."

"I think it'll work," Bostwick said. Millicent nodded in agreement.

"Very well. Let's see… so we only need some magical twig or something, but then, how would we get close enough to actually touch her? Touch is needed for mechanomagic, you know."

"Sounds like you've already got a plan. Don't tell me you inherited Lesserian magic from your father but you've been keeping it a secret this whole time."

"Don't be absurd. Ancient Styx magic is so powerful there's no room for anything else. Well, except floating, but that hardly takes any effort at all. Anyway, how would said Lesserian get close to her? Surely Alcea would kill anyone who tried."

This statement settled over everyone like a chill in the air. Emmaline squinted off into space while Bostwick took out his pocket watch and calculated the time left until he had to face Alcea.

"She'll have to stand still if she wants you to turn her shadow into an immortal beast," Millicent said quietly, "but… to try and trick her… It's too dangerous."

"You did exactly that last night," Bostwick said, "without any backup."

"I couldn't do anything else! And she didn't find out about my plan. If she had…"

"And yet," Delilah said, now emitting a slight purr, "*tricking* her may be our best bet. Our only bet. She keeps harassing us, so why not do what magicians do best and turn the tables on her? Drive her away for good, just like what happened with the Empire long ago. She wants human magic? We'll give her a show."

She marched to a shelf beside the bed and retrieved several pieces of stationery, then slapped them onto the table and began writing.

"I'll trust you to make this sound more official, Emmaline, and to make sure it's full of loop-holes, but how about *this* for a contract?"

She held it up, beaming with pride, for all of them to see. Emmaline and Millicent read it over with confused and pitying expressions, while Bostwick grimaced.

"And to think," he said, "after that speech you just made about magicians, I thought you actually might have begun to respect me a little."

"But I don't understand," Emmaline said as the queen shoved the make-shift contract and the rest of the paper over to her. "How is this supposed to help with Alcea?"

"Like this."

Delilah removed two black objects from her pocket: the halves of the Domino of Nonpareil. The cut edges glistened blue in the dim light. "The poor thing has been out for the count, but there's still some magic left in it."

"Can you fix it?"

"Of course."

"Then why haven't you?" Bostwick asked.

She held the broken mask up before her and looked through the two eye holes at each person in the room.

"I wanted to be absolutely sure that I needed to. My ancestors gave up a lot to create this mask, you know? Styx's honor was at stake. But now that my dear butler is as well… Well, I think it's worth it."

She took a seat on the ground with her legs beneath her and held the two halves of the Domino so they touched. A few blue sparks sizzled at the cut. Delilah took a deep breath and summoned her glowing energy spell between her two hands while still holding the mask. It grew brighter and brighter, flooding the room with white light so that the humans had to look away. Finally, the light faded.

Delilah held, in one hand, the Domino of Nonpareil, whole once again.

"Well, that was easy," Bostwick said.

"My skill just made it look that way." Delilah hovered a foot off the ground. "Oh good, I *can* still float. I'd really have been heartbroken if that went away."

She landed clumsily, laid flat on her back, and put the restored Domino onto her face.

"Are you all right?" Millicent asked, rushing over to her.

"Just tired. I think I'll lie here for a while." She held her hands above her and stretched her fingers. "Hmm. Weird."

"What's weird."

"Nothing actually. I just wanted to know if it really worked, and it did. I can't use my ancient Styx magic anymore, you see. It's all in here." She tapped the mask.

"That's how you fixed it?" Bostwick asked, horrified. "You transferred your magic into it?"

Delilah crossed her hands over her stomach and explained. "As you know, Bostwick, magic is turning will into reality. That's what the Domino does, by using numerous people's magic as a source for greater power than any single goblin would have. When I say that this is my family's mask, I mean it contains the powers of my family, literally."

"Delilah…"

"Say nothing, Bostwick. If you're willing to face an immortal beast head-on in order to give us a tiny window of opportunity for beating her, I'm willing to do whatever it takes to get through that window."

"But you're in no condition to be running around turning into who-knows-what!" Millicent said, helping Delilah off the floor and to the bed. The queen walked awkwardly, and fell rather than climbed onto the mattress.

"Hmm… I suppose you're right, Millie, but still, the show must go on."

Emmaline read over the contract she had just rewritten, comprehension dawning on her face.

"It will!" she cried

"Hmm?"

"Let me do this, Delilah. Your father explained how mechanomagical invention worked to me, and I've used the Domino before. And I… I'll take good care of Bostwick and the Domino. I'll bring them both back safe and sound."

"It could be risky, you know," Delilah said, handing her the mask anyway. Emmaline took it carefully, knowing what it contained.

"Well… you know what they say: 'Noblesse, No-blige'."

"They do say that, don't they?"

All through the night, Emmaline and Bostwick worked on the plan, recruiting Misha to help them with the principles of shadow magic. He had also brought the all-important element of the top hat, specifically the tiny green one that

Danika had kept hidden from the police and palace guards even after the more dire warnings about Alcea went into effect.

Only the queen had managed to sleep, with Millicent keeping a nervous watch over her. Other than a drained sort of exhaustion, Delilah didn't seem any worse after giving up her ancient magic, but Millicent still refused to send her down to talk with Sebastian, telling Cecil that she was "indisposed" and would see him when she was feeling better.

"He says it's really, really important," the guard said, returning for the third time. It was only a few minutes before nine o'clock.

"I suppose we can't leave him meowing down there all day," Delilah said with a yawn. "I hate to miss the proceedings with Alcea, but you'll all just have to make do without me."

"I'll go with you," Millicent said. "I'm still not sure you're okay."

"But Sebastian said to come alone," Cecil said, but Delilah waved him away with her hand.

"I'm the queen and I say what goes. However, Millie, are you sure you don't want to stay here?" She nodded towards Bostwick and Emmaline, who were still talking with Misha about their impending mission. "Hmm?"

Millicent shook her head, but fidgeted for a moment, so Delilah called out, "*Bost*wick, come here at once!" When he came to her, she jutted her thumb at Millicent, then dragged Cecil away toward the door.

"Um…" Millicent said. "Just… be careful."

"I will," Bostwick assured her.

"Right. Well, um…"

She threw her arms around him and buried her face in his shoulder.

"Don't worry," he said, hugging her to him. She responded with an unabashedly worried noise, but managed to smile at him anyway as she pulled away. After she left with Delilah, Bostwick checked his watch and noticed that his hands were shaking.

"Don't worry," he repeated to himself.

"It's just about time," Misha said as Emmaline donned the mask and transformed. "Ready?"

"Not really," Bostwick said, "but it's not like we can stop now."

Misha turned into a wispy shadow and wrapped around Bostwick. The magician's vision went black and he felt for an instant like he was floating in a void. A moment later, he felt solid ground beneath his feet again. The blackness faded, revealing a field of blue and gray; it took Bostwick a moment to realize he was seeing the sky and seashore. He sat, feeling nauseous, and noticed that there were thin white grasses growing all around them.

"This is where I harvest daft stocks for memories," Misha said. He picked up the big gray top hat they had materialized out of and handed it to Bostwick. "Don't worry, though. They don't collect memories until they're cut and dried."

"You came," said a voice from above them. A raven circling overhead landed and turned into Alcea. "I had my doubts. You may go, Misha."

Misha glanced at Bostwick, who shrugged, then left through the hat. The magician then removed the contract from his pocket and handed it to her.

She glanced over it, smirking. "Really?"

"Yeah. I just… I've never been able to do it. Just that *one* spell. And you were a teacher at the Academy, so you should be able to explain it."

She transformed into Hollyhock and took the hat from him, then scrutinized the inside. "Pulling a rabbit from a hat is not unlike conjuring a handkerchief or a flower, though it's slightly more complicated, due to its animal body. Just as more complex restoration spells require a container to focus a magician's magic, so do more complex conjuration spells."

"But what about conjuring shadow goblins? That doesn't require a container." He honestly wanted to know, but he also wanted to give Emmaline as much time to prepare as possible. He, at least, still felt woozy and not entirely ready for their plan to be set in motion.

"Alistair didn't conjure anything," Alcea said. "He merely transformed a shadow into a goblin. The image of that goblin existed, and the shadow was already present, as much as a shadow can be."

"But he still created a goblin from practically nothing. I mean, that's the whole point, isn't it? You want to create life from nothing."

"I just want to create life. I don't care where it comes from, as long as I have a hand in it."

"But… why?"

"Why do *you* want to pull a rabbit out of a hat?"

He couldn't tell if she was being evasive or if she truly saw no difference between those two desires. Either way, he wasn't going to let such a question slide.

"To prove to myself that I can," he said, standing unsteadily. "That's not a reason to toy with someone's life."

"And yet, here we are. Aren't we?" She said it like a threat. Bostwick couldn't stall anymore.

"Well, I don't really care about your reasons. I'm just here to learn how to do the rabbit trick. So… the hat focuses my magic, and I just…"

"You will a rabbit into that space where there was no rabbit before." She reached into the hat and pulled out a small white rabbit, then replaced it. It seemed to require no more effort than breathing. "Now you try."

He took the hat and looked into it, hoping with all his might that the plan would work. He reached in, counted to ten, and then pulled out a fluffy brown rabbit. He breathed a sigh of genuine relief and set the rabbit down onto the ground. He was about to reach in again, but Alcea—as a shadow goblin—took his hands with her shadow and forced him to kneel at her feet.

"One thing before we begin: if you try to double-cross me, I'll order Sebastian to start killing people… So you were planning something," she said when Bostwick winced involuntarily. "Humans never seem to grasp that you can't trick someone with thousands of years of experience. And so you don't feel overly confident, be aware that I have removed Sebastian's restraints. Now, shall we begin?"

"How… how do I know that you won't kill them, or me for that matter, afterward?"

"You'll just have to trust me."

"No."

"No? You're in no position to…"

"I want a guarantee. I want to know why it is that you won't kill me as soon as I cast the spell. You must fear that I might turn the new shadow goblin mortal." Alcea merely tossed her head, as if the topic wasn't even worth discussing. "Fine, then," Bostwick continued, hoping Emmaline could figure something out on her end. "I'll tell you what my plan to double-cross you was, if you tell me why you'll let me live."

The immortal beast's eyes took on a hungry look. She was still a collector at heart, and information of that sort was probably something that she rarely had a chance to bargain for.

"Well, we are all alone here," she said, gazing at the windswept grasses around them. "You promise to tell me your plan if I tell you my secret? Bear in mind that your friends' lives are not part of this bargain, and can still be forfeit."

"Right," he said, staring up at her.

She knelt in front him and whispered almost inaudibly. "I made a promise, long ago, never to kill anyone." She stood up once again, all the while keeping Bostwick's hands pinned to the ground.

"But… but what about the bomb?"

"Danika set it."

"But you were going to send Sebastian after…"

"He would be the killer, not me. Don't look so surprised; you know how I like to use loopholes. So… you'll be safe out here, as long as you do what I ask. But first, tell me what your plan was."

"Right," Bostwick said, more disturbed now, knowing about her so-called promise, than when he thought she could murder him on the spot. "First of all, that's not my signature on the contract. Delilah just wrote my name on it, so it's not legally binding."

"I suspected as much, but that's irrelevant. We still made a deal and I carried out my part of it."

"Actually, I knew all that about the rabbit trick already. I've still never been able to do it. Even this time, I never magically pulled a rabbit from the hat. She was up my sleeve the whole time."

"Up your slee—?"

In a swirl of pink and brown, the heretofore forgotten rabbit that had been hopping innocuously beside Alcea transformed into a short Lesserian goblin with curly, magenta hair. She seized the immortal beast by the arm and said, in a single breath, "I wish you'd leave Styx and everyone in it alive and in peace."

Alcea lifted her shadow off the ground to strike at her, but Emmaline had already turned into a shadow goblin and swirled into her smoky form. She curled around Bostwick, as they had practiced the night before, and sped through the top hat back to Chiaroscuro.

"Sebastian," Alcea spoke into the air, knowing that he would hear her through the contract, "apprehend one of the humans to use as a hostage."

If Bostwick refused to be rational, then she would just have to drive a harder bargain. He might not have been as easy to manipulate as Millicent had been, but he still didn't seem like the sort to let an innocent person die.

Alcea already knew that following them through the hat would be useless, as they must have planned to destroy it on their return. She turned into a bird to fly to the city—but instead fell to the ground, still a shadow goblin. She tried to transform again, but nothing changed. She stared at the spot on her arm that Emmaline had touched, and saw a strange, peacock-and-black-colored lump on her arm. It felt hard to the touch, like a stone.

Sebastian paced his room, hoping that Delilah would deign to meet with him soon. He had been so nervous that he had only caught a few minutes of sleep here and there. Augustus lay dozing on the sofa, while the Empress stood with her back to the door.

"She's probably doing this on purpose," he said, "just to torture me."

"Being royalty can be a busy job," the Empress said stoically. "I remember."

Sebastian still didn't know quite what to make of her, so he kept pacing in silence until, finally, the door opened and Cecil, Delilah, and Millicent stepped through.

"I want to talk to you alone," he told the queen.

"I think I'll be all right now, Millie. You really ought to go up and welcome back Bostwick and Emmaline. Now what was it you needed?" she asked after Millicent and the shadow goblins, save Augustus, stepped out of the room.

"Our deal. You need to do it now."

"It?"

"You have to kill me."

"What an audacious statement! I don't have to do anything."

"You said you would… Please. I don't want to be forced to…" It was agonizing being unable to tell her the truth.

"*Did* I say I would?" she mused. "Then I suppose I've changed my mind."

"Listen! This is…" He took a calming breath, trying to think of something the contract would let him say. "You need to kill me. It's… important."

"Well, it's also important not to rush these things, you know. Didn't you want to say goodbye first? I'll have you know that Bostwick and Emmaline are out risking their lives while you're in here trying to throw yours away."

Whatever she was referring to, it must have had something to do with Alcea. Though he knew they couldn't win against her, he was reminded of Millicent and Bostwick's assurances to him the day before. For a moment, he hoped that they had, by some miracle, convinced her to leave, but then his mind was flooded with Alcea's voice. *Sebastian, apprehend one of the humans to use as a hostage.*

He was too late.

Without a word, he walked out past Delilah and shoved Cecil and the Empress out of his way. Millicent was just on the other end of the ambulatory, and had not yet ascended the stairs.

"Millicent!" he called, unable to audibly finish with *"Run!"*

She turned and walked back to him to see what he wanted, and he grabbed her by the arm.

"What's going on? Why…?" She placed her hand against his shirt, eyes widening as she realized he was not wearing the beffudlium, and tried to pull away without effect.

"Sorry," Sebastian said. At least, he thought, he had

received no further instructions.

"It's okay. But where is she? I thought she was supposed to be in the Wastes."

By this time, Delilah and Cecil had joined them. The queen unhelpfully smacked Sebastian across the face, crying, "Unhand her, you cur!"

"It's the contract, Delilah! Don't slap him!"

"Well, what am I supposed to do? It's not as if I can use ancient magic to defend you. I feel so useless. Is this how humans feel all the time?"

Alcea's voice drowned out the rest of their conversation. As Delilah pushed Millicent out of his grasp and got between the two of them, Sebastian heard, *Actually, Sebastian, kill the human. They need to know I mean business.* Though everything in him rebelled against it, he raised his shadow up to slice through her. As he did so, however, Delilah threw both arms around him. With one final heave, she pulled him over the rail of the ambulatory where they fell together, down into the open atrium.

Thirteen

Sleight of Hand

Several floors flew past Sebastian's eyes, but before he could understand what was happening, Delilah had already slowed to a gentle float and shoved him roughly away from her. He fell the last ten feet, hitting the floor hard. His entire left side ached from the impact. Still, the contract had to be carried out and he managed to stand, wincing from the pain in his leg. He morphed into his shadow form and leapt up to the second story landing, then the third. He was vaguely aware of Delilah yelling something from below him as he climbed back up, but she could only float so high, it seemed.

When he arrived back to the floor Millicent was on, he saw Cecil standing protectively in front of her.

"Leave this to me," Cecil told her. "I've been trained in combat."

"But—"

"Do what he says!" Sebastian said, lashing at her with his shadow. Cecil countered with his own, giving Millicent time to run back toward the southern staircase. Sebastian made an attempt to get past him by turning into a shadow once more, but the guard again used his own, this time throwing

Sebastian back against the wall. He sat for a moment—his left arm was already bruising from the fall, and he could only imagine what shape his leg was in—until the contract made him stand again.

"S-sorry, Your Majesty," Cecil said.

"You're just doing your duty. I'm the one who should be apologizing," Sebastian said, throwing a punch which the guard easily blocked.

"Well, it's that spider lady's doing, right?"

Sebastian nodded.

Though the contract was forcing him to try every means of getting past Cecil in order to kill Millicent, including trying to slice through his chest, it was clear that he was entirely outmatched by an official member of the Chiaroscuran Order of Law, contract or no. His injuries weren't making it any easier, either.

"Are you all right, Your Majesty? You don't look so good."

Cecil leaned forward and Sebastian reluctantly stabbed him in the foot. While the guard screamed and dropped to the floor, Sebastian ran past him in the direction Millicent had gone without having time to apologize. He had almost reached the stairs when he heard, *Go to where the nearest hat is, Sebastian.*

Having disposed of the one in his chambers long ago, he only knew of one hat inside the palace. He shadowed down several floors to the Document Chamber. The guard outside saluted him, giving his bruises a curious glance, then unlocked the door at Sebastian's request. Inside, a top hat lay cut into two pieces on the table. Having no further instructions,

Sebastian asked the guard to lock him in, hoping that might at least slow him down if he was given the order to kill again. He gathered the hat in his hands, then took the opportunity to rest on the floor.

Tell me, have you reached a hat?

"Yes," he said to the empty room.

Hold the pieces together to make it whole again.

Once he did so, Alcea issued out of it. She shook where she stood, clutching her arm as if she'd been wounded.

"Did you manage to kill that human?"

"No," Sebastian spat.

"Good. Now that I've had a moment to think, hostages may still prove to be useful. Bostwick's companion sealed this into me." She removed her hand to reveal a discolored, raised patch of skin. "I'm going to make her take it out. Which one of them was using the Domino?"

"None of them. I cut it in half."

"They must have fixed it. Didn't they tell you what they were planning, why they stuck me in this form? Tell me what you know."

"I heard that Emmaline and Bostwick were risking their lives somehow, but that's all... You really can't change shape?"

She began to pace around the chamber, not answering his question.

"It must have been Emmaline, then. Ah, yes, the one who wrote the contract. So that was their plan... What should we do, Sebastian?"

"You're honestly asking me for advice? You just ordered me to kill one of my friends, and now—"

"Friends? That's exactly it, Sebastian. Up to now, I've been shooting in the dark, trying to figure out what to trade these people, how to use them. But you *know* them. If I wanted to convince Emmaline to remove this wishing stone from me, what should I do? Bargain with her? Threaten her?"

"Maybe if you hadn't given her a reason to fight you in the first place…"

"*Tell me* how to make Emmaline remove this stone. Who does she care about most?"

"That would be Mr. Charles, Bostwick, and Millicent—and Delilah, inexplicably. But threatening them won't make any difference. As long as you can change shape, you're a threat to this city. Emmaline would never forfeit the people's safety for any one person. I learned that in Styx a long time ago."

Alcea pondered this a moment.

"Really?"

"You know I can't lie to you. The contract makes it so."

"In that case, what should I do? Tell me."

"Leave Styx," he said defiantly.

Alcea stopped pacing and crouched down in front of him. "Tell me what to do in order to get one of the others to use the Domino to remove this stone."

"I'm not sure that Bostwick or Millicent would be willing to do it either, knowing how dangerous you are, and that you might kill both of them in the end anyway, but Delilah…" He tried to stop, but the words kept coming. "She never thinks things through, and she's selfish."

"And?" Alcea said, leaning towards him. "Tell me how to get to her."

"Threaten the people she cares about. She'll do anything for them."

"And those would be the three humans? Answer." Sebastian nodded miserably. "Very well. Once you leave this chamber, kill whichever human you get to first, and capture whichever human you come to after that."

"But if we just threaten them…"

"I already told you, Sebastian, that we need them to understand how serious I am about this. Seeing one of her humans die will give the queen incentive to listen to my request."

Alcea knocked on the door and the guard opened it. He looked confused as the two of them stepped into the hallway, but he still saluted Sebastian just the same.

After meeting Bostwick, Emmaline, and Misha on her way up to the royal chambers, Millicent insisted they go back to help Cecil. When they reached the ambulatory, they found him on the ground with the Empress holding his foot up, clutching it tightly between her two hands. Despite what was apparently an effort to stop any bleeding, the guard's boot was still soaked in blue blood. Sebastian was nowhere in sight.

"It's a mere scratch," Cecil said, despite the tears running down his face.

"Here," Emmaline said, turning into a plain brown box using the Domino. Bostwick hesitated, then instructed Cecil to put his foot inside and began to cast the spell.

"This is… weird," Bostwick muttered.

"As if anything to do with goblins makes any sense!" said Emmaline's voice from the box. "Just hurry up with that spell."

"Where's Sebastian?" Millicent asked Cecil when it seemed like the pain had subsided.

"He went down to one of the floors below. I lost sight of him."

"At least that'll give us some time to figure out what to do," Bostwick said. "There. You should be fine now."

Cecil extracted his foot with a look of wonder on his face. "Good as new! Magicians are amazing!" He hopped up and began to flail around, then swooned back to the floor.

"You still lost some blood," Emmaline said, turning back into a human. "You should probably rest for a bit."

They helped him back to the bedroom, where Augustus was just waking up. He seemed unfazed by the fact that Sebastian was not among them.

"Why the long faces?" he asked with a yawn.

"The king has been possessed," the Empress replied.

"Or at least he's being controlled," Bostwick said. "I knew Alcea was clever, but I never counted on her actually figuring out that Sebastian was wearing beffudlium beforehand. How easy is it to get more, Cecil?"

"The armory's on the bottom floor, but a lot of guards carry handcuffs."

"I wonder..." Emmaline said, closing her eyes in concentration. "Hmm. I guess you can't use the Domino to turn into beffudlium. I could go back to being a shadow goblin, but if Sebastian managed to injure a trained guard, I don't know how much help I'll be."

"We can at least be on guard," Misha offered. "You, Augustus, and I… and what about *you*?"

"Ghosts are no good at fighting," the Empress said.

"Then you should stay with Cecil. Anyway, we'd better hurry before Sebastian's ordered to attack anyone else."

After peeking into the hallway to be sure they would not be ambushed, the two magicians made their way out onto the ambulatory, surrounded by the two goblins and Emmaline, in Chiaroscuran form. Misha led them towards the staircase, which was the fastest way to the lower floors. They went slowly, keeping their eyes out for any signs of movement.

As they passed the last room before the stairs, something black shot out from the darkened doorway. It was aimed at Millicent's head, but Bostwick saw it a second beforehand and shoved her out of its way with his arm.

His scream echoed across the atrium as the shadow swiped neatly though his wrist. The goblins faced the direction the shadow had come from, where Alcea and Sebastian turned from their smoky forms to their normal shapes, but Millicent was too shocked to move.

Blood from Bostwick's wrist was pooling on the floor and there, over by the wall, lay—

Millicent's vision blurred, and for a moment she was sure she would faint, but Emmaline had already pulled her and Bostwick onto the staircase. Millicent could hear sounds of fighting happening on the ambulatory, but she couldn't comprehend what was going on. Bostwick slumped on the stairs next to her, taking shallow, sobbing breaths.

"Here," Emmaline said, returning, though neither Millicent nor Bostwick had realized that she had left them.

She handed Millicent Bostwick's right hand—the one that had been severed—and changed into a box around his wrist. Millicent shook her head, clutching his hand to her chest.

"It has to be you, Millicent! He's in no position to cast a spell."

"I'll mess it up," she sobbed. "It might never heal properly."

Bostwick grabbed her right hand with his left and said, through teeth clenched in pain, "I'll help you."

Millicent nodded, placing his right hand inside the box. "I-I'll try."

Sebastian watched Emmaline drag the two magicians away, grateful that at least one person had the presence of mind to get them to safety. Though the contract was forcing him to fight his way towards them, Misha and Augustus together were providing enough of a challenge to give the humans a chance to escape. A moment later, however, and Emmaline came back, crawling along the ground. She picked something up off it, and Sebastian felt his blood run cold.

He'd been so focused on fighting, and so relieved to see Millicent and Bostwick get away that he hadn't thought for a second about what he had hit while still hiding with Alcea in the darkened room. Now he noticed, as he continued to slash at his opponents, the stains of blood on the floor leading away to where Bostwick had been pulled by Emmaline.

"This is taking too long," Alcea said, sweeping her shadow under Misha's feet. She curled it around them and flung him through the air. He would have gone right down into the atrium if Augustus hadn't leaned over the rail and grabbed him just in time. Though they were both safe, they were no longer in any position to defend the humans.

"Come, Sebastian."

Alcea walked to the staircase and pointed at it, as if to signal to Sebastian where his duty lay. Only a few steps down, Bostwick and Millicent sat, staring into a box with looks of revulsion on their faces.

Though Alcea's command to kill the first human he came to still stood, he tried with every ounce of strength to fight against it. He'd been ordered to kill before this, but actually seeing the familiar crimson of human blood splattered on the white tiles of the palace brought everything back to him. Red on white. Blood in a snowy courtyard. He couldn't bear doing something like that again, but there was no way out. He raised his shadow over Millicent and Bostwick, who looked helplessly up at him, then…

He turned, placing his body between them and his shadow. Alcea's command still stood, but this wouldn't be suicide. He didn't *want* to die, but he had to protect his friends.

At least… I won't become a murderer, he thought and brought his shadow down like a blade.

When it was an inch from his face, it blinked out of existence; only a shimmering light was left in its place. Behind him, Bostwick and Millicent were holding their hands up together. His left and her right completed the spade-like shape of the shadow vanishing spell.

Sebastian's surprise, relief, and disbelief were all short lived, as he spun and kicked out at Millicent, narrowly missing her face. The box that had been around Bostwick's hand changed suddenly into a wyrm, which pressed Sebastian to the ground with its huge clawed feet. He couldn't move, no matter how much the contract told him to.

"Let's make a deal," the wyrm said.

Alcea had not moved an inch since Bostwick and Millicent had vanished Sebastian's shadow. She still stood at the top of the stairs, clutching the wishing stone in her arm.

"Deal?" she asked haughtily.

"A simple one. If you cancel Sebastian's contract, we'll let you leave the city."

"I'll only cancel it if you remove this stone and the wish from me."

"Since we're the ones who can seal your shadow magic any time we feel like it and then lock you away in beffudlium for the rest of your life—however immeasurably long that may be—you're in no position to negotiate. Not to mention the fact that we've got you surrounded."

She pointed her long snout behind Alcea, where Augustus and Misha had their shadows at the ready.

"You drive a hard bargain," Alcea said, eyeing the people all around her. It was obvious she was looking for an escape route.

"I had a good teacher. Now, do we have a deal?"

Alcea looked Emmaline in the eye, and Emmaline stared back, unblinking. Finally, Alcea shrugged.

"Very well. Sebastian, disregard all the orders I have previously given you."

"Don't trust her," Sebastian said. "The contract is still inside me. I can feel it."

"Then don't feel it," Alcea said, and swiped her shadow at Emmaline, who ducked. Misha and Augustus both ran to apprehend the beast, but she had already turned into a shadow and arched backwards over their heads and down onto another floor. Misha followed her, while Augustus merely leaned against the wall and took several deep breaths, muttering something about not being cut out for this line of work. No one else said anything until Misha returned a minute later.

"She went into the Document Chamber," he said. "I think she used the hat inside it somehow."

"Well, I guess I can let you up," Emmaline said to Sebastian.

"Wait. I need some way of warning you about Alcea if… If I hear any more orders from her, I'll call her Hollyhock."

"All right."

She turned back to normal, and the two of them, plus Misha, sat around the magicians. Millicent was still crying, and Bostwick looked grim. He held his arm tightly around her shaking shoulders, but his hand and fingers sat at odd angles and looked as if they had been crippled.

"I'm sorry," Sebastian said to them after a moment.

"It's not your fault."

"No, I mean… I'm sorry for… back then… in Styx."

Bostwick sat up in surprise, then mumbled, "Um… I—"

"I am *so* sorry!" Millicent cried before he could finish.

"What? Why?"

"Y-your hand!"

"It's fine. I'll just re-heal it later."

"But I…"

"Listen," he said, leaning his head on hers, "considering how much I bled in that short amount of time, if you hadn't… It could have been a lot worse. You did just fine."

"But how did you two know to do the shadow spell *together?*" Emmaline asked, hoping to cheer Millicent up. "That was brilliant."

The magicians looked at each other and shrugged.

"We panicked," Millicent said with a sniff. "I mean, we were already holding hands, and when I saw that you were going to kill yourself…" She glanced at Sebastian. "…I just raised my hand instinctively, and Bostwick and I both just sort of knew what to do."

"Neither of us could do it alone," Bostwick explained, "but together, we had enough magic. It must be like the Domino, using more than one person's power."

"The Domino?" Sebastian asked.

"Yes, the Domino!" cried a voice from down the stairs. It was Delilah, trailing a dozen guards carrying armfuls of beffudlium. "It's good to see that everyone decided to sit down and take a break from immortal beast hunting. Where is she?"

"She left," Misha said. "But it would be a good idea for you to wear beffudlium for a little while, Sebastian, just in case she comes back."

"I want him coated in the stuff!" Delilah declared. "Now let's see. Emmaline, you've taken excellent care of the Domino. Good. I see that Sebastian did something so unseemly that he offended Millie's delicate sensibilities and caused her to burst forth into tears. Just what I would expect from one such as him. And… Why, Bostwick, your hand…" He gestured across his neck with his good hand, signaling for her to let the matter drop, but she just smirked. "You finally defended Millie's honor. Well, it's about time."

Millicent looked at him questioningly, but he just shook his head and said, "For once, it's really better just not to ask."

Fourteen

Justice and Punishment

After several uneventful days, Alcea had still not shown up. Sebastian again warned the Council and the palace guards about her, this time describing her in detail so they could be sure of what she looked like, in many of her different forms. A week after the incident, the Council declared yet another party—this time a citywide festival—in celebration of the defeat of a dangerous immortal beast. After two hundred sixty years of hiding, they were ready to celebrate anything they could.

Bostwick, unfortunately, could not freely enjoy the food and festive spirit, because he kept being mobbed by Chiaroscurans as he and his friends walked through the lantern-lit streets.

"You're that magician!" A blue haired girl squealed, dragging him up onto a table. "Do some tricks! Do some tricks!"

"Um… sure. Well, for my first trick, I'll need a volunteer."

Several young shadow goblins elbowed their way up to him. Delilah looked on with a smirk, eating fried dumplings off a stick. Her expression was only slightly obscured by the Domino.

"You didn't have anything to do with this, did you?" Millicent asked.

"I *might* have started a rumor that Bostwick *might* have saved the king's life with his magic."

"Then why aren't they asking me to do tricks?"

"You'd get stage fright, Millie. I didn't mention you."

"That is sort of a relief, but I wanted to spend time with Bostwick during the festival."

"Leave it to me," Clarence said, fighting his way through the crowd and leaping onto to the table. "You've seen some amazing tricks, ladies and gentlemen, but are you aware that the man who stands before you is *also* a poet?"

"What?" Bostwick asked, turning pale.

"It was our second year at the Melieh's Academy of Magic, and I learned of his gift for the poetical arts. But there was no place for a heart such as his, for all the poetry contests that year had already passed. All, save one: The Imperial Society of the Black Lily, an all girl's organization! Though Bostwick protested—"

At this point, Bostwick shoved the handkerchief he had conjured into Clarence's mouth, as the shadow goblins looked on with a mixture of confusion and amusement.

"I'm not sure that necessarily helped anything," Emmaline said, though Bostwick did manage to leave Clarence behind on stage; the other magician made a show of removing a whole line of colored handkerchiefs from his mouth, continuing the magic show to let Bostwick escape.

"Never, ever ask about that contest," Bostwick muttered

when he got back to the rest of them.

"We won't," Millicent said.

"*Ever.*"

She laughed and twined her fingers through his. His hand was back to its original state, though he had refrained from mentioning to her that it required one of the Chiaroscuran doctors to sever it once again so he could heal it properly.

"Of course," Delilah purred, "we can all guess what such a situation would have entailed on your part, Bostwick. Perhaps, if you write a ballad extolling my many virtues, I'll arrange for that unpleasant memory to be removed."

"Don't look at me," Misha said. "I've sworn off leeching out memories for good. I'm going to focus on my duties as a royal steward… although I'm still not sure whose steward I'm supposed to be."

"Mine, of course. Hands off, furball!" She grabbed Misha around the neck and pointed a finger accusingly at Sebastian, who was still wearing a beffudlium belt and collar, and a bracelet of the metal on each wrist.

"I would think that would be up to him to decide," Sebastian said.

"Nonsense! You have no idea how to employ a Misha of this sort. While he was running around as your fetch-and-carry boy, I was busy having him relay vital intelligence about Alcea. If he hadn't brought me his memories, the map piece, and Millie, none of this would be here right now, in several senses. You really should thank me."

"He *should* thank Misha," Millicent said.

Delilah shrugged and released the ex-memory merchant, then wandered off to acquire yet more food. Sebastian watched her go with an annoyed scowl, until Millicent nudged him in the arm and flicked her eyes in Misha's direction.

"Um, thank you," Sebastian said.

"N-no, I was just doing my job!" Misha said, waving his hands in front of him. "And it's not like I could just let Alcea get away with her plans. Or you with yours, either, right?"

"My plans... Right."

Sebastian bit the side of his finger and Misha continued to fidget. Their silence was growing more uncomfortable by the second, and everyone was grateful to see a guard in a resplendent red uniform with a gleaming silver sword and scabbard strutting purposefully toward them. It took them a moment to realize that it was Cecil.

"Miss Maid, look!" He pointed to the sword, which was embedded with a glittering sapphire in the hilt. "They only give these to people who have done a great service to the city. The Council commended me for my injury in the line of duty! It's only been eight days since I started; they said it was a record for that kind of thing."

Bostwick wondered if the record referred to the length of service or the glory of the injury, but the guard had already run off to tell more people of his accomplishment.

"Doughnuts!" Delilah said, appearing with an armful. "I even got one for you, Ex-Four Paws O'Meowly."

Sebastian took the paper wrapped doughnut without a word.

"I wouldn't eat that if I were you," Bostwick said.

Delilah gasped and cried, "Why, whatever do you mean?"

"Just that you probably put something weird in it."

"Hmm... Define weird."

Sebastian had already put the doughnut in his pocket anyway, and was now gazing at the brightly lit food stalls and smiling goblins around them with a dazed look.

"Are you okay?" Millicent asked.

"I'm fine. Just thinking."

"You mean sulking," Delilah said, giving his braid a yank. "Well, since you're so good at it, I suppose I'll allow it just this once, but tomorrow I'll need you in a less Sebastianesque mood. There is still one tiny little overlooked detail we must discuss."

The following day, Delilah waited with Millicent in Misha's room, where Sebastian joined them.

"What's this about?" he asked, facing them as they sat on the sofa.

"Surely you know. I've seen you sulking around ever since Alcea left. You're still thinking about the matter of your punishment, aren't you?"

"Oh." Millicent deflated. "I thought that maybe you'd changed your mind about that."

"No. We had bigger things to deal with, but now that Alcea's no longer in the picture, I can finally make up for my crimes." He bent his head as he spoke, biting his index finger.

"Hmm?" said the queen. "What's this? Weren't you practically begging to die before?"

"I… I deserve to…"

"But you don't want to?"

After a moment of thought, he shook his head. "It's not just a matter of knowing how painful it is," he said, holding the spot on his wrist where he had cut himself before. "After seeing everything the Ancient Shadows worked to build, and meeting all of you… knowing what you were willing to go through for me… I don't want to throw it all away."

Millicent beamed at him, but he went on.

"But it doesn't matter what I want. I *deserve* to die."

"Hmm," Delilah said. "And I suppose, as your darling queen, it's up to me to pass judgment on you. Very well, then. For betraying my butler, kidnapping Millie, consorting and contracting with an immortal beast, endangering the map of Styx and the city of Chiaroscuro, and for attacking everyone and their uncle—under the influence of the contract or not— and for ruining my dress—don't you dare think I forgot that—I… pardon you."

"What?" Sebastian and Millicent said in unison.

"That power also lies with the queen," Delilah said smugly. "I promised Millie that I'd let you live, after all, plus I really don't feel like killing anyone at the moment."

"That's wonderful!" Millicent cried, throwing her arms around Delilah. Sebastian was less enthusiastic.

"You're forgetting my most serious crime: Inez died at my hands. Whether it was her or Alistair makes no difference. I still intended to kill somebody."

"Hmm, yes. You even wanted to kill me, if I recall; only your ineptitude at magical combat and my amazing skill saved my life. You really won't be satisfied unless you receive a proper punishment, eh?" Delilah stood and walked to the window, where rain poured down on Chiaroscuro. "You really risked a lot for this city, even if your original intention was to weasel out of the contract through suicide."

"Changing the subject isn't going to help at a time like this," Millicent said. "Unfortunately."

"I'm doing nothing of the sort, Millie." She floated over to Sebastian and leaned back on one hip, looking him over. "You really love your people, don't you?

"Yes," he answered simply.

"And you really have bonded with my darling butler and maid, haven't you?" He nodded. "In that case, you are hereby banished from Styx, including Chiaroscuro."

"Banished?" he asked, turning to her with a troubled expression. Delilah stared steadily back at him, raising an eyebrow. After thinking it over, his shoulders slumped. "I… I suppose I could accept that as a punishment."

"But Delilah…" Millicent began.

"It's better than execution, isn't it? And I'll make sure you're given sufficient funds and clothes and such. And we'll remove your beffudlium. Can't have you dying out there."

"Out there?" he asked, sounding drained. "Ataxia?"

"I meant the Empire. I think you'd fit in more with humans than goblins."

"I agree," Millicent said, working up a smile. "And… and you can start over. You don't have to worry about the past."

"Plus, Alcea probably won't follow you that far," Delilah said. "Not that she'd follow you at all. I'm just, you know, being cautious. Anyway, the one stipulation for this punishment is that I expect written correspondence on a monthly basis, or I'll send Bostwick to track down your mangy hide and drag you back to Styx."

"Wouldn't that defeat the point of being banished?" Sebastian asked, a hint of annoyance returning to his voice.

"Not at all. If you can't be decent enough to write to us, I'll just turn you back into a cat and mush your ears and pull your tail and never give you a moment's peace!"

"I'll write," Sebastian said. Delilah smiled. There was an understanding between them, even if it was a not entirely friendly one.

Millicent stood with her hands folded in front of her, looking in turns at Sebastian and the floor. Eventually, she sighed, squeezed her eyes shut, and threw her arms around him. He stumbled back against the wall.

"I'm going to miss you," she said. "I'm glad you won't be executed, but I didn't want you banished for life!"

"For life?" Delilah cried. "Chaos, no! I never said anything about life!"

"Then how long?" Sebastian asked.

"Until I feel like it. Maybe when you crawl into my throne room on hands and knees, singing my praises and begging to be let back in. Maybe sooner, maybe later. I'm not totally heartless."

Millicent hugged Sebastian again and said, "She's really not, you know?"

While Delilah called Millicent away to "discuss things" with Sebastian, Emmaline and Bostwick went to the palace's entrance hall to say goodbye to Clarence and Dolly.

"Sorry about my messenger pigeon not working out," Dolly said, hoisting her stick and bindle over her shoulder. "Naturalistic magic's not always reliable when it comes to animals."

"Well, we managed to survive, anyway," Bostwick said. "So, are you going back to your tribe, or are you still technically dishonored?"

"I'm not really sure about the honor part, but after traveling aimlessly and then hearing about the plight of the Chiaroscurans, I've decided to make it my goal to spread peace and understanding throughout the world. No one should be forced to live in a crumbling shadow or be enslaved to another person."

"Or be controlled by a love potion."

"O-or that. It doesn't matter if it's someone who hatched from an egg, or was born, or was created through magic. Even the shadow goblins deserve their moment in the sun… weather permitting," she added with a glance to the downpour outside.

"I'm sure you'll make a great orator," Emmaline said. "Just remember, there's no such thing as false tea."

"You said that before. What does it mean, anyway?"

"I don't think it actually means anything, but I kind of think it could apply to what you were talking about."

"Well, we better be off," Clarence said, putting his jackalope on his shoulder. "I want to get a hat from Rare and Priceless before we leave the country. It's not that I don't love Jill, but she's a bit unwieldy to carry around. Which reminds me, Bostwick, did that beast end up telling you anything interesting about pulling rabbits from hats?"

"Nothing I didn't already know. I guess it's just something I'll never be able to do."

"Or that you just have to keep working on!" He turned on his heel to race out the door, but stopped mid-step and wheeled around again. "Ah, but there was one thing I wanted to ask about. Whatever became of my magic carpet?"

"Delilah unraveled it."

"I suppose it couldn't have been helped," he said with a shrug.

"No, it really could have."

"Anyway, I guess we'll have to get to the town on foot, so we should probably head out."

He and Dolly waved goodbye and Bostwick turned to Emmaline.

"So… What about you, Emmaline?"

"Me?"

"You're not a rabbit anymore, and Styx is safe, so…"

"I've been thinking about it. I'd definitely like to help Chiaroscuro with their infrastructure now that they have to deal with weather and darkness and such, but I also have a duty to the Empire, as a princess of Camellia."

"So what are you going to do?"

"I don't see why I can't do both." She had a very Delilah-esque expression, and Bostwick once again wondered if spending so much time with goblins was really a good thing for her.

"Well, whatever your scheme involves, it… it'll be weird not having you around."

"I'll miss you too, Bostwick. But you might end up seeing me more often than you think."

"Why can't you just tell me what you're planning?"

"Because I'll have to talk with the empress about it first… The real one, not the Chiaroscuran."

"Yeah, I got that," he said, following her back up the hall.

Fifteen

The Nopali Desert

The Nopali Desert was nothing like Sebastian had imagined. It was hot and arid, of course, but it was also teeming with life and color. Bushes and cacti climbed over every ridge and flowers dotted the hills along with scrubby, light green grass. The train he rode on turned and traveled into a canyon, so that the window on the exterior of his compartment showed nothing but flat white rock, while his own window looked out on the opposite canyon wall, which was a rainbow of earth tones and textures.

As breathtaking as all of this was, Sebastian found it hard to concentrate on anything but the letter he held in his hand. He had been traveling the Empire for months, never staying in one town for more than a few weeks, yet somehow this letter had found its way to him.

He had finally arrived at Millicent's hometown, South Wellington, a lush area far from Styx's border, in hopes of discovering more information about Alistair. The townspeople could offer him none, preferring to stare at him, unabashed. He was used to such a reaction by that time, though humans seemed to be less and less surprised by him, as he had seen several groups of goblins during his stay in the Empire's larger cities. It seemed that travel was becoming popular in Ataxia.

After spending the day in a futile search for answers, the last thing he expected was recognition from the receptionist at the desk of South Wellington's only inn.

"Ah, so you're that goblin? I was wondering when you'd show up. Someone left a letter for you."

He handed Sebastian the letter without further comment. It read:

To Sebastian, the Ancient Shadow (if you are not him, please excuse this and return it to the desk),

I have some information you may find valuable, and there are matters we must discuss. I have enclosed enough currency to purchase a ticket for the Intercontinental Imperial Express, Route 27, South Wellington to Nopalito Station. If you would meet me on the ten o'clock train, it would be much appreciated. Simply leave this envelope with the porter, with the date you intend to meet me, and I'll see you there.

Though Sebastian found this exceedingly suspicious, especially given that there was no signature, his curiosity got the better of him. He left word with the receptionist, then bought a ticket for the following morning.

He had been on the train for half the day already, traveling through a juniper forest and finally to the Nopali Desert, but no one had approached him yet except a young female conductor who blushed when her fingers grazed his as he handed her his ticket. He felt trapped in this compartment, even more so now that the only way off the train would be a fall down the canyon wall.

He breathed slowly, trying to remain calm. Perhaps

Delilah was trying to contact him for some reason, and enjoyed putting him on edge. And surely, he told himself, Alcea wouldn't follow him to the Empire.

He was about to read the letter for the twelfth time that day to see if there was some detail he had missed when the compartment door rolled open and a well-dressed, middle-aged human stepped in and took the seat across from him. He leaned over, shut the door, removed his hat, and stared out the window with an amused smile.

"Don't you just love trains?" he asked.

Clearly, this man was just another passenger and had nothing to do with the letter. Sebastian wanted to ask him to leave, but there was no polite way to do so.

"I do," the man continued. "All machines, really. Just this morning I saw three motorcars outside the train station, and Emmaline is hoping to get airships in the Capital by next year."

Sebastian felt as if cold water had just been thrown on him, but thought it best not to betray any emotion. The man laughed at his confusion.

"You have no idea who I am, do you? Good, good. I would have signed my name to that letter, but it would have been troublesome if it fell into the wrong hands. Speaking of which, you are Sebastian, aren't you?"

"You already know who I am," he replied coolly.

"Well, of course. But I wouldn't want to tell all this to some random shadow goblin. That would get confusing. Anyway, I'm Mr. Charles, former tea inspector of the Principality of Camellia. I believe Emmaline mentioned me once or twice?"

"What do you mean by 'former'," Sebastian asked, warming slightly after learning that the man was the tea Inspector that Emmaline had spoken so highly of.

"Ah, you see, after Emmaline came home to us, safe and sound, she explained that her quest to become human had awakened in her a newfound sense of duty. First, she went to the empress to explain the matter of Chiaroscuro and the shadow goblins…"

"Are they all right?" Sebastian asked, unable to contain his curiosity. He hadn't heard any news of Chiaroscuro in months.

"They're just fine. As part of Styx, Chiaroscuro is in alliance with the Empire. Many imperial mechanics are already being sent to help with the city's infrastructure: glass windows, lights, and all that. As I was saying, Emmaline made sure that was all taken care of. She's going to spend a bit more time with her family, but then she will become the first official Ambassador to Ataxia, to foster trade, good will, and migration."

"So that's why I've seen so many goblins around."

"Something like that. Apparently, the Queen of Styx's travels have had some fascinating effects on goblinical sentiments. There have been several requests from the K'nick-k'nack Tribe to work out a sort of student exchange program, some visitors from Catawampus—if you can believe that—and even a few shadow goblins coming over the border to the Capital.

"I'm very proud of Emmaline," Mr. Charles continued. "She has become even more resourceful and responsible than she was when she left Camellia, which is saying something.

She's turning out to be an amazing young lady."

He smiled dotingly for a moment, then cleared his throat and pointed a gloved hand at Sebastian.

"But you asked about my job, didn't you? Well, as much as I love tea, inspecting it has become a bit dull, so I've decided to branch out in my negotiations. I'm going to accompany Emmaline to Ataxia this time. Exciting, isn't it?"

Sebastian was pleased to hear news that Emmaline and Chiaroscuro were doing well, but he couldn't help but feel that this information was meant as preliminary small talk to more important matters. And something still bothered him.

"How did you know to leave that letter in South Wellington?"

"Emmaline told me about your beginnings and your, let's say… motivations, so I assumed that you would want to find out about the people who created you."

"So you knew I would be in Alistair's hometown?"

"Yes, or to be exact, where you thought his home town was. It turns out that Alistair was a native of the Capital, born to a wealthy family of doctors. He moved to South Wellington later in life. After everything Emmaline told me, I did a little digging. I know all sorts of people with all sorts of information."

"So that's why you sent me the letter."

"Indeed, but I really wanted you to see this." He gestured out the window. They had come out of the canyon by now—though the train was still on elevated ground—and could look out over rows and rows of flowering fruit trees, leading away to a distant mountain range. It was as if the entire desert had been taken over by orchard.

"The Bustan Orchard," Mr. Charles said. "The Bustan family pioneered many irrigation techniques to increase the yield of fruit crop. It was through their efforts that the entire Empire is regularly supplied with cheap and delicious fruit... or at least that's what it says in the pamphlet." He handed a printed piece of paper to Sebastian, who looked at it blankly. "They give these to tourists, you see. It goes on to say that this land has been in the same family for hundreds of years, and was even home to the renowned Inez Bustan."

Sebastian read the words over in the pamphlet several times, then asked, "Was she her mother? I mean, the mother of the Inez I knew."

"What? No, no you misunderstand. That *is* the Inez you knew."

"Maybe Emmaline didn't explain everything," Sebastian said quietly. "Inez died before I was sent to Styx. I... I killed her."

"So we thought, but as I told you, I did a little investigating—"

"There's no point in pretending it didn't happen. I was there."

"But the Bustan family can provide documents to prove what I'm saying, and then there's the history boo—"

"And how do I know I can trust you? If you really know 'all sorts of people', couldn't you find someone to provide false documentation?"

"You bring up a good point, but—"

"I appreciate what you're trying to do, but I know what happened."

Mr. Charles tilted his head left and then right, as if

weighing something in his skull, then sighed.

"So you really won't take my word for it?" he said, removing one of his gloves.

"No. Now if we have nothing more to say, I'll find another compartment."

"One moment. Let me just… Ugh, this is so gauche."

Before Sebastian could stop him, he placed his ungloved hand on Sebastian's forehead, took a breath, and concentrated.

Mr. Charles walked up the stone path to the Bustan house, breathing in the smell of creosote bushes and hearing the buzz of cicadas. He removed his top hat when he stepped into the cool shade of the covered porch and knocked on the heavy wooden door. It would all have been rather pleasant if not for the peculiar circumstances which brought him there. After several minutes of waiting, a woman with sleek black hair and copper skin wearing an opulent red dress swung the door open, smiling, but stepped back when she saw his magician's garb.

"You're from the Academy?" she asked, with suppressed anger in her voice.

"Yes. Mrs. Bustan, I presume?"

"Yes," she answered curtly.

"I am Mr. Charlemagne Rhoswen, President of Melie—"

"It's been two years since anyone from the Academy contacted us. What could you want now?"

Mr. Charles let the woman's barely concealed ire wash over him, straightened his cravat, and continued.

"I received a letter from one of our former students asking me to… look in on your daughter. I was hoping to speak with her, if she's well enough."

The woman stared down her nose at him, and for a moment he wondered if she wouldn't just slam the door in his face. Finally, she stepped back to let him in.

"She's probably out in the orchard. You can wait for her here."

She offered him no food or drink, which didn't surprise him. He had not been amongst those magicians who accompanied the severely wounded Inez on her long trip home, but he could imagine the horror her family had gone through when they had been told about what had transpired—under the nose of the then-President Folio—at the Academy. He was honestly shocked at how civil Inez's mother was being to him, under the circumstances.

Not knowing when Inez would arrive, he settled in and surveyed the room, which was surprisingly cool, with large windows, dark wooden furniture, and jewel-tone painted walls. Along with inheriting the fiasco of the students' experiments, which had taken months to sort out once he and the Empress managed to oust Folio from his position, he also received the president's old office and had been looking for ways to make it feel less bleak.

He pulled out his pocket watch to check the time when a pale boy began to walk through the room, but stopped dead in his tracks at the sight of the president, balling his only hand into a fist.

"Alistair," Mr. Charles said with a nod. "I received your letter."

"You…? But I sent it to the Academy."

"Of which I am now president. The situation you talked about seemed urgent, so I decided to come and see these 'experiments' that Inez is performing with my own eyes. But since she isn't here, might I ask how you came to live with her? Doesn't your family live in the Capital?"

It had been bothering him since he first received Alistair's letter, since he did not usually mix up facts about mortals, and couldn't see how the son of the Empire's best doctors—doctors who, from what he was told, had saved Inez from the very brink of death with a groundbreaking human-to-human blood transfusion procedure—would end up in the Nopali Desert with the family of the girl whom he had almost gotten killed.

At first, Alistair looked as if wild horses could not drag a response from him, but after a moment he collapsed onto the sofa beside Mr. Charles's chair.

"My parents… disowned me."

"Well… that… that's not right."

"Isn't it? They said what I had been doing was the same as human experimentation, that it was like tying down a person and cutting them open." He shuttered and clutched what remained of his right arm with his left, then whispered, "I think they were right."

Mr. Charles could think of no words of comfort, and any satisfaction he might have had at Alistair's all-too-late epiphany was eclipsed by learning his family circumstances.

"So…" he asked, "you came to live here?"

"I wouldn't have dared ask that of the Bustans, after what happened. No, Jurek took me in."

Jurek Jablko, one of the other students who had participated in the experiments: Mr. Charles had met him only once, after the inquisition of the other students and the creature named Sebastian when he and the empress had gone to the Academy infirmary to find Inez clinging to life by a thread, attended by Alistair's mother, father, and brother. Jurek had occupied the other bed, recuperating from having provided the blood for the transfusion. In Mr. Charles opinion, it was a miracle that either of them had survived.

"I'm still a bit confused, Alistair. If you lived with the Jablkos…"

"Then why am I here? Because of the experiments—"

"*The* experiments?"

Alistair glanced away. "Not exactly. I didn't think anyone from the Academy would come if I told the truth, so I made it sound like what Inez was doing was connected to the shadow experiments. But I promise, what she's planning is just as dangerous."

"Is it?" a female voice said.

Inez, in a wicker wheelchair pushed by Jurek, had just entered the room. She wore a dress similar to her mother's, though her left arm was in a sling.

"You know it is," Alistair muttered, "even if you won't listen to reason."

"And you thought ratting us out to the Academy would change my mind?"

"You mean convince you not to kill yourself?"

"No one's killing anyone *this* ti—" she began, but doubled over in a coughing fit. Her two companions appeared concerned, but not alarmed; it seemed that this was a typical aspect of her condition. Mr. Charles cleared his throat.

"Perhaps we should all begin at the beginning, and save the arguing for later? So, Jurek, you and Alistair went to your home in…?"

"Cliftonshire. We were both expelled, and Alistair… Well, my family runs a small farm, and there's always work to do, so…"

"With one arm?"

"I… didn't really think that part through."

"I pulled my weight using magic" Alistair explained. "Most jobs requiring heavy lifting can be accomplished through levitation, and restoration spells work on farm equipment just as well as pocket watches. But I also came up with new spells, to make life a little easier with only one hand. I sent my notes to Inez, too, so she could use them. But when she wrote back, that's when the trouble started."

Mr. Charles turned a raised eyebrow on Inez, wondering if she might want to explain her part in whatever these new experiments involved, but she was still catching her breath. Alistair continued.

"Inez had been working on magic too, only her theories were much more ambitious than mine. She wrote to us that she intended to perfect biological restoration."

"Not a bad idea," Mr. Charles said, "considering how hit-or-miss it's been so far."

"In theory, it's great. The problem is testing it."

"You never seemed to think… that was a problem before," Inez shot at him through labored breaths. Alistair paled, but Jurek stepped in.

"We both know you're planning to test it on yourself. That's why we came down here, President Rhoswen—to talk her out of it."

"And I suppose that didn't work." Mr. Charles tilted his head. "So you wrote to me about it so I would use my Academical authority to stop her?"

"Well, Alistair did, but…"

"But?"

Jurek looked to Inez as if asking for permission for something. Inez nodded at him, and he left through the door they had come in through.

"But you've convinced him," Alistair said, answering the question that hung in the air, "that you can actually heal your injury."

"Isn't it at least worth trying?" Inez asked, unloosing her sling and letting her arm fall onto her lap.

"It's not worth risking your life. *He's* not worth—"

"This isn't about Sebastian." She spoke so quietly that Mr. Charles almost didn't hear her. She wheeled her chair slowly over to the table and used her right hand to lift her left onto the tabletop and carefully fold it into a fist with only the thumb sticking out. "I want to see him again, someday, but this isn't about that. I almost died that night, Alistair, and you almost killed someone, and it all started because we couldn't rely on box healing. I don't want anyone to go through that again."

By this time, Jurek had returned with a tiny paper box; it was spotted with dark brown and red in some places.

"Why paper?" Mr. Charles asked, watching Inez conjure a kitchen knife, then carefully slide the box over her thumb.

"It's easier to cut through."

He raised an eyebrow. Though not the most skilled at biological restoration himself—even immortal beast had their foibles—he had sat in on a number of healing classes. The procedure had always been that students would make small cuts, then stick the wounded body part into a wooden box in order to concentrate their magic. Paper boxes would be more useful to bring with one out in the world, but surely, she wasn't planning…

"Inez, Wai—!" Alistair cried, but she had already lifted her knife and slammed it down with a deafening chop.

Mr. Charles slowly sat back down—he had apparently jumped to his feet without realizing it—and examined Inez's hand. The knife was had clearly sliced through her thumb and the box that surrounded it, but there was no blood.

Inez wrenched the blade out of the table and brought it into the air; it was spotless, as was her intact thumb, once she removed the two have of the box from around it. Alistair stood, gape-mouthed, and though Jurek had obviously seen this spell before, he too, had a wide-eyed, stunned expression. Inez slowly sighed, as the spell must have required her complete concentration. The three former students, still processing what had just been done, seemed to form a tableau of surprise and relief. Mr. Charles, having a few years on them, recovered first.

He applauded.

"A most excellent trick, Miss Bustan. I assume you have replicated it."

"About ten times now. But only ever on my fingers, and only on this hand." Brushing back her hair, she muttered,

"I'm not sure if it hurts or not, since I can't really feel anything… But I intend to keep trying. Once I'm sure I can do it perfectly on my left arm, I'll move onto my right."

"And keep going from there?" Alistair said. "This doesn't change anything, Inez. Your end goal is still the same, and it's still likely to get yourself killed."

"Not if my theories are sound. I didn't even try that spell until a few weeks ago. Before then, it was all in my head."

Alistair clenched his jaw, then turned to Mr. Charles. "Can't you stop her?"

"I'm afraid I am inclined to agree with her. Miss Bustan, what you're doing may well beckon in a new era in biological restoration, but you are aware that it will be more challenging from here on out. Fingers are just bones, skin, muscles, and joints, but should you continue in your plan, you'll be dealing with all manner of delicate organs, not to mention scar tissue. Frankly, you are lucky to be alive as it is."

"Exactly!" Alistair cried, jumping up and pointing at Jurek. "He saved your life, Inez. You owe it to him not to do this."

"Well, she saved yours," Jurek said, "so if we're talking about people owing anyone anything, you should probably help her with this spell. If anyone could figure it out, it would be you two."

From what Mr. Charles had heard in bits and pieces from the faculty at the Academy, this was likely true; Inez and Alistair had been the best students in their year, and if they had come up with a way to make Hollyhock's immortal-creation scheme into a reality, they might be two of the most gifted magicians alive. But Mr. Charles knew that what Jurek suggested was unlikely to come to pass. Alistair looked now as he had on the night of the inquest: dark eyed, haunted, afraid of his own shadow—or other people's, perhaps. He had already seen what he thought was his friend's death once, and was essentially being asked to aid in that again. That, and he no longer had any family to turn to. While Inez might one day heal herself with magic, it would take much more than that for Alistair.

"Ah, well… perhaps we should leave the theorizing to Miss Bustan," Mr. Charles said, straightening his cravat once again. "You've a ways to go before you'll be needing a second person to cut you open, so we needn't worry about who that is at the moment. Meanwhile, Alistair, I'm curious about your non-Capital relatives. No one was originally from there, so you must have someone…"

"I have an Uncle in South Wellington, but we barely know each other."

Perhaps that's a good thing, he thought, mentally making a note to track down this uncle once he left Nopali. Surely something could be arranged. He did, after all, know all sorts of people, with all sorts of information.

As for Inez, he wasn't worried about her. The spell was dangerous, but he had a feeling that Jurek might end up staying with her as she perfected it. Of the three of them, he seemed to have the most common sense, fetching teachers on the night that Alistair and Sebastian had started to square off with each other, and then demanding that Alistair's parents be contacted for Inez when magical healings methods failed. He had not let her die that night, and he doubted he would do so now.

♠ ♦ ♣ ♥ ♣ ♦ ♠

Mr. Charles replaced his glove without a word. He frowned at the tears that ran down Sebastian's face and silently handed him a handkerchief. Sebastian held it in his palms and pressed them against his eyes for several minutes, then stared out the window, biting the side of his index finger.

"So, she was very much alive," Mr. Charles said. "You're lucky, you know. I really hate showing people the past. It just seems so…"

Sebastian nodded, then jumped in his seat.

"You're an immortal beast!"

"You figured it out. Well done. Now, back to the matter of Inez."

Sebastian settled back and bit his finger again.

"What happened to her after that? Did she ever…?"

"Heal herself, well, not exactly, or entirely. It took years for her to even completely master the technique on her fingers—apparently doing it on an arm with working nerves hurt *a lot*! But she didn't give up on it, and eventually became so skilled that she could actually heal her fingers so seamlessly while cutting through them that she felt no pain. She wrote about the theory behind it, but although I was the president of the Academy, I never really understood restoration much. It's not really my cup of tea.

"But I digress. The more complicated the system, the more willpower and understanding needed to do a proper spell, and to make it easier on the caster, Inez moved from using a swift knife movement to a slow sawing motion.

Sounds grisly, but I'm told she could heal so well that it didn't even tickle. By this time, we were teaching her technique to the Academy faculty, and from there to the students. It was about, oh, ten or fifteen years after that that she finally felt that the spell was, as she put it, perfect, and asked the Empress's court magician come to the Nopali Desert to try the spell on her torso."

"Did it work?" Sebastian asked, afraid to hear the answer, and taken completely aback when Mr. Charles hit him on the head with the pamphlet about the orchard.

"*If* you had read this you would know the answer. This orchard is home to the renowned Inez Bustan, the first woman to be sawn in half via magic. Of course, she wasn't sawn in half with magic, she was *kept* from being sawn in half with magic, actually, but people like to sensationalize things for the tourist. And it wasn't as 'in half' as your standard trick nowadays, which goes right through the middle. No, they started with her shoulder, since it was still a delicate area, but not so full of vital organs. And it wasn't actually a success at first…"

"I don't… need to know all the details." He steadied his shaking hands, looking out over the orchard to try and clear his mind from the images in his head. "Just… was she all right? In the end?"

"Well, she survived, if that's what you mean, but she never was able to heal the wound completely. See, magicians generally restore one wound at a time, so to fix something like that, that has, more or less, already been healed, however badly, means that you have to either reopen the whole wound at once—which really would have been fatal in her case, if the spell went wrong—or go incrementally, cutting a small, damaged area and healing, then moving on to the next, and the next. They only ended up 'cutting her in half' so to speak, about a dozen times before she thought that maybe it was enough. In those days, it was still a risky procedure, and she had a family to think about by then. She ended up quite a bit healthier, but not enough to travel, so…"

"So?"

"That's why she never went to see you in Styx, if you were wondering."

He hadn't been. Half an hour ago, he had thought that she had died a painful, bloody, needless death in the Academy courtyard. To find out just the opposite was more than enough for him. There was one thing that still bothered him, though.

"If… if you knew Inez was alive, why didn't you tell Emmaline, so that she would tell me?"

"Oh," Mr. Charles said, sounding thoroughly surprised at the suggestion. "Well, from everything I knew of your situation before, I suspected your actions were merely a form of vengeance against Styx for imprisoning you. It wasn't until Emmaline came home and explained the entire situation to me that I realized your mistaken perception about Inez was fueling your self-loathing. Even if I had known, I must say that I figured that you would have gotten over it after two hundred years."

"I would never have 'gotten over it'!"

"You say that now, but trust me, people change given centuries. Alcea didn't used to be nearly so wretched. If you hold onto unpleasant ideas all that time, it's bound to mess with your way of thinking. And anyway, it doesn't really change anything. You still attacked Alistair, Inez still got in the way. The fact that she didn't die is inconsequential."

"If that's what you think, then why did you bother telling me?"

"Because I know mortals. To you, it changes everything."

"It does change everything! To know that Inez didn't die, soaked in her own blood… That she got to grow up, and have a family… Her healing spell saved Bostwick's life! It's probably saved countless lives!"

Mr. Charles muttered something that sounded suspiciously like "inconsequential", but smiled and said, "I'm glad I brought you such good news. How about some more, concerning Alcea?"

Sebastian could feel his heart beat faster. He nodded for the immortal beast to continue.

"Somehow or other, Alcea knew that I had mentored Emmaline, so she came asking me to remove the wishing stone from her in exchange for your contract. I, of course, refused."

"But why did she even go to you in the first place? Do all immortal beasts… That is, would you really be willing to help her?"

Mr. Charles leaned back in his seat, as if settling in to tell a story.

"Long ago, when she first started to despair about not being able to create, I'd promised her that I would never turn away from her, and that I would always listen if she came to me, so long as she promised *never* to kill anyone. You see, she was already becoming obsessed and vindictive, even going so far as to bargain with people for their children. None of the other beasts wanted to have anything to do with her, convinced that she would start deliberately orphaning people next. I thought I could help her, but I never imagined that she would do anything like she did with the Ancient Shadows.

"Anyway, when she came to me a few months ago, she wasn't in her right mind. Once it became clear that I would never remove that wishing stone, no matter what she offered, she seemed almost desperate to get rid of you, like a bad memory. In the end, she traded me your contract in return for the rest of my Aureate Tea Set, which I have had for five centuries. I traded her part of it long ago—in exchange for her sitting for a portrait—and she's always had her eye on the rest. It's very old and very rare. To tell the truth, I was a little sad to part with it."

Mr. Charles finished and became absorbed in staring out the window. Sebastian contemplated what he had said for a moment.

"She traded me… for a tea set?"

"Well, half a tea set… Which means she either values that tea set a lot, or values you very little. Either way, her priorities are just a bit mixed up, aren't they? But like I said, she was desperate. I don't think she's ever *lost* to anyone before. She'd take whatever she could get, if you know what I mean."

"So then, I have to serve *you*?"

"That's why you came to the train station, isn't it? My note told you to come."

"So it wasn't just curiosity…"

"Sorry about that. I'm not a fan of controlling people, but

I really did want to explain things to you. Now, if the second party of the contract, that's me, was to forsake the protection of Chiaroscuro, that would break the deal, but I prefer to makes things more 'concrete' shall we say?" He took a blank sheet of paper from his pocket and held it up to Sebastian. Without needing to be told, the goblin placed his hand on it.

"Come on out now," Mr. Charles said. Ink bled out of Sebastian's hand and onto the paper, reforming the words of the contract in Alcea's handwriting.

"Now what?"

"Now you see it," the tea inspector said, casting a small flame spell and lighting the edge of the contract on fire. Both men watched as flame slowly ate up the paper, which Mr. Charles dropped onto a tray he had taken out of his hat for the occasion. In a matter of moments, it was nothing but ash. "And now you don't."

"You're a magician?"

"When I'm a human… not that anyone alive now knows that. Anyway, just to be sure that the contract is null and void, slap yourself on the face." Sebastian merely raised his eyebrows in disbelief. "Good, good. That's all settled, then."

"For me it is, but what's to stop Alcea from attacking Chiaroscuro, now that she has no vested interest in protecting it?"

"First off, it's not her style. She has nothing to gain from it, and there isn't much she can do as a lowly shadow goblin." Sebastian scowled at him, but the immortal beast waved his hand dismissively in the air. "Take no offense at that. I mean low compared to her previous powers. Shadow goblins are no different from any other creatures, no matter how their race began. After all, there's no such thing as false tea… It's a secret metaphor, you'd never understand it."

"That aside, she could still go after any magician to make them do what she wants."

"Not as public enemy number one, she won't."

He held up a large paper with a picture of Alcea in her shadow goblin form drawn on it. Written underneath it was a brief description of her behavior and abilities, as well as a warning to stay away from her and to contact an Imperial authority if she was spotted.

"These are going up all over the Empire as we speak. Hand drawn, with a near perfect likeness, if I do say so myself."

"Do you really think these posters will be enough to protect people?"

"Alistair's spell for sealing shadow magic is also being taught to all magicians, including the students of the Academy, and the Empire's police are being outfitted with befuddlium. Everyone will know Alcea for what she is and be on guard. And she still has to keep her promise to me not to kill anyone… personally, at least."

Sebastian said nothing, simply staring out the window.

"But I've been rambling, haven't I. The point is, Alcea is used to relying on trickery and deception. That will be a lot more difficult to do now that the entire Empire can see her for what she is. It's not exactly just desserts for everything she's done, but I feel it will at least keep her at bay."

"I hope you're right," Sebastian said.

♠ ♦ ♣ ♥ ♣ ♦ ♠

The train soon stopped at a small station near the orchard. The smell of citrus blossoms that wafted towards the platform was almost overpowering. Sebastian exited the train car and stared out at the trees, picturing Inez sitting under them, maybe reading one of her many books, or practicing a less dire magic spell than—

"Ah, and one more thing," Mr. Charles said, interrupting Sebastian's thoughts. His head was sticking out the window of the train. "If you ever tell anyone about what I am, well, let's just say that I've found you once, I can find you again. And I never made the promise Alcea did."

He finished this barely-veiled threat with a smile, then pointed toward the ticket office.

"Oh, look. Anyone you know?"

Sebastian turned to see Augustus and the goblin who referred to herself as the Empress—the former in what looked like a chimney sweep's attire, the latter in high collared pink dress and carrying a parasol—standing at the ticket window arguing with the man at the desk. Sebastian looked back at Mr. Charles, who gave him a thumbs up, then walked toward the two shadow goblins.

"It's no good, Empress," Augustus said. "We just don't have the dough. It looks as if melting or burning or what-have-you is inevita—Oh, hello then," he said, spotting Sebastian. "Your Majesty, or ex-Your Majesty, I suppose. What are you doing here?"

Sebastian was about to answer when he realized that he wasn't entirely sure himself. This morning, he had been wandering in search of answers, but now that he had them, he didn't know what to do next.

"We wanted to buy a ticket," the Empress said before Sebastian could say anything, "but we don't have any money."

"We spent it all getting here. We were on a sightseeing tour," Augustus said, then lowered his voice. "Actually, the Empress nicked a jeweled statue on the way out of the palace, so we decided to get as far away from Chiaroscuro as we could instead of going back to prison. Unfortunately, the area we currently find ourselves in is becoming hotter by the day. I think there must be some disaster coming."

"It's getting closer to summer," Sebastian explained.

"Oh, is that it? Still, I've been told by the locals that it will soon be unbearable, so I suggested to the Empress that we leave but, as she said, we're low on funds."

"I couldn't help over hearing," Mr. Charles called from the train window, "but did you say you are low on funds? I could help you out. I'm from a noble family, you see, so I have money."

"He shouldn't squander his heir's inheritance," the Empress said to Augustus.

"I don't think he'll mind," Mr. Charles said, waving a wallet at them.

Augustus rushed over, grabbed it with a hasty word of thanks, and ran back to the ticket window.

"So, Empress, where to?"

"Where to?" she asked Sebastian.

"Oh, I… Do you want me to come with you?"

"If that's what you want," Augustus said, scratching his stubbled cheek.

Sebastian considered it. He no longer owed allegiance to

Alcea, nor was his life controlled by Delilah or the students of the Academy. And he had no more plans concerning his city, his people, or even the end of his existence. For once in his life, he did not know what the future held.

"We could go… to the Capital." He had avoided the city on his entrance to the Empire, finding the thought of his memories there too painful. But now, seeing those memories in a new light, he wanted to revisit the city of his birth.

"I suppose things will have blown over in Chiaroscuro by now," Augustus muttered, turning to purchase their tickets. "And if it comes to it, you can probably pardon us."

"Probably not. I'm not technically a king anymore."

Augustus shrugged, muttered something about breaking out of prison once and doing it again, and paid the cashier.

"Hmm?" he said, grabbing an overstuffed trunk with his shadow and scanning the train windows. "Where'd that rich fellow go? There's still a bit of money in this wallet."

"He turned into a bird and flew away," the Empress answered, looking up at Sebastian, "right?"

"Er…"

"Don't mind her," Augustus said, leading the way to the train. "I'm sure we can find him somewhere inside, and if not, hey, free money, right?"

"Right," Sebastian said, noticing a bluebird watching them from a branch of one of the lemon trees. He nodded to it, then boarded the train behind the other two Chiaroscurans.

Sixteen

All's Well That Ends...

"Gross incompetence! Skullduggery is what I call it!" Delilah cried. "How do you expect to explain yourself, Emmaline?"

The queen, the princess, and Mr. Charles sat in the upstairs library in Styx Castle. Emmaline had decided to stop by Styx to say hello to her friends before starting her ambassadorship to the other Ataxian countries, only to have Delilah drag her upstairs, saying that she would be detained until Styx received "satisfaction".

"Well, first, I would need to know what you're accusing me of," Emmaline said, taking the situation in stride. "But before that, I brought the letter you want—"

"I'm accusing you of causing the disastrous situation in Chiaroscuro. Not you personally, of course, but since you've chosen the woeful path of ambassadorship, the weight of the Empire's crimes falls on your shoulders."

"Crimes?"

"Of which there are too many to count! The Chiaroscurans have developed a habit of walking into the glass windows the Imperial technicians have installed, and no one bothered to tell us that electricity was dangerous. The shadow goblins made quite a game of swinging off those wires until one of them got shocked. He's lucky to be alive."

"We didn't think anyone would *swing* on them."

"Well, you should have thought of that," Delilah continued, sipping her tea demurely. "After that incident, a rebellious faction of the citizenry was absolutely convinced it was some sort of Imperial experiment to fry them all. They chopped out half the wires in Chiaroscuro with their shadows. The city was without light for a month."

"So *that's* what happened," Emmaline said. "Back in Camellia we heard reports of widespread panic in Chiaroscuro. If that's all that caused it, it will be easy to sort out. But that aside, shouldn't we give this letter to Millicent? President Willfrock insisted that I deliver it to her personally."

"What are you, a mailman?" The queen grabbed the letter from Emmaline's hands, snatched up several other envelopes from a nearby table, and threw the entire pile out the library window. "*Bost*wick! Mail!" she shouted, and slammed the window shut. "Now, where were we?"

"Skullduggery," Emmaline said with a sigh.

"Ah, yes. Well, you can see the trouble your lack of foresight has caused my poor citizenry."

"Well, considering that our own citizens have been dealing with the influx of goblin tourism and the increased chaos that came with it, I think we're even. However, I do have a good-will offering for you, if you aren't too upset with the Empire to accept."

Mr. Charles held up a wicker animal carrier.

"A present from the Empire," he said. He opened the door of the carrier and brought out a chocolate-brown, lop-eared rabbit and handed it to Delilah, who seemed to melt back into her chair as she brought the rabbit to her chest.

"Thank you, Emmaline!" she squealed.

"I made sure it was a brown one especially," Emmaline said. "Just make sure to take good care of him. It's tough being a rabbit, you know, especially in Ataxia."

"I shall do my best. His name shall be Flop-ears St. Bunny of Bounceton Manor, heir to the forty-carrot fortune of—"

An explosion from the floor above them brought her description to an end, and blue smoke started to waft down outside the window.

"It's only Danika," Delilah explained. "I said she could come and do her chemistry in our laboratory. I figured that would be safer than in Chiaroscuro, where a single collapsed building might bring down the whole city. Besides, my grandfather used to do much more dangerous experiments up there. See that reddish stain in the ceiling?"

Before she could continue her story, Misha stumbled in, covered in a thin blue dust.

"Everything's fine," he coughed. "Danika managed to contain most of it in her shadow before it ate through the glass."

"I'm just going to pretend I didn't hear that," Delilah said, then gestured to Emmaline and Mr. Charles. "We have visitors, Misha. You remember Emmaline? And this is her chaperone, Mr. Charles. And *this* is Flop-ears St. Bunny of

Bounceton Manor; 'Reginald' for short."

"Right," Misha said, staring blankly at the rabbit.

"Danika is not allowed anywhere near him. Who knows what would become of the poor fellow? I guess I can let Bostwick use him for pretend hat tricks, though."

"Speaking of which," Emmaline said, "Can I finally go see him and Millicent, or am I still being 'detained'?"

"Detained? But we're allies! Anyway, Millie and Bostwick are practicing magic in the garden," Delilah said. "I was about to go see them when you came. I always need to give Millie Sebastian's letters."

She pointed to the bare table, frowning in confusion, then bent down to check under it.

"You threw it out the window."

"Ah, of course," she said straightening up.

"How's Sebastian doing, anyway?" Emmaline asked tentatively.

"It's difficult to say, as his letters are all rather short and to the point. They mostly say something to the effect of 'Millicent, I found Kibwe's name on a plaque somewhere,' or 'I thought I was going to die, but it was actually just hay fever.' Still, Millie seems to enjoy them."

"And there hasn't been any sort of... trouble?" Emmaline said.

"For all I know, he could be running amok as we speak, but he hasn't written about that in his letters. So far, anyway. Still, I'm curious to see what he'll say in this latest one. I'll be right back. Here Misha, you hold Reginald."

♠ ♦ ♣ ♥ ♣ ♦ ♠

"Her insanity continues to reach new heights," Bostwick said, sorting through the letters that had fallen from the window. "Some of these could be important."

He took a seat beside Millicent on the picnic blanket, which held a basket, a plate of cheese and apples, and their two upturned top hats.

"Oh! There's the Academy crest," Millicent said. "It must be for you."

Bostwick looked the envelope over and handed it to her.

"No, it's for you."

Millicent checked the addressee just to be sure, then carefully opened the envelope and pulled out a single sheet of paper, tilting her head to the side as her eyes traveled over the page.

"I guess… since learning the origins of the personality test, President Wilfrock and the empress have decided to cancel my results for it. And it says it'll still be given to future applicants, but more as an evaluation tool instead of an absolute bar to admittance." She looked over the letter once more, turned it over, then returned it to its envelope. "I don't know why he sent it to me, though."

Bostwick recalled the day, last fall, when President Wilfrock himself showed up at Styx Castle to personally apologize for having barred Millicent from the Academy. Millicent had explained about her current situation and her desire to stay in Styx, no matter what became of the personality test, and Wilfrock had apologized once again anyway, commended Bostwick's decision to become her tutor, and had left the matter there, or so they thought.

"Maybe they're sending it to everyone who failed the test,

as a customary measure. Of course, I still think you're the only one, but…"

Millicent nodded, magically stowing the letter in her small yellow top hat, then folded her hands in her lap. "Anyway, where were we?"

"Mechanical restoration," Bostwick said, taking out his pocket watch. "All you need to do is break this watch, put the pieces in your hat, and then fix it using magic."

Millicent nodded again and Bostwick passed her his watch.

"So I just… smash it?"

"Technically, you're supposed to conjure a mallet to destroy it, but if you throw it at the ground the first time, just to break the glass and maybe the lid, you can get a feel for repairing it."

Millicent stood up and flung the watch at the ground with a morbid expression, watched it bounce twice, then picked it delicately back up.

"Oh, I hope it works," she said, fiddling with the lid that hung at a right angle to its hinge. She placed the broken watch into her hat, moved her hands over it, and reached in. She pulled out something that looked like an inside-out machine hanging from the chain, with springs and gears sticking out all over.

"Oh no!" she said, looking at the watch as if it were a small animal she had wounded.

"It's okay. This time, don't try to think about it so technically, just—"

"Why, that's my watch!" Delilah cried, bounding over to them and snatching it from Millicent's hands.

"It's *my* watch," Bostwick said, taking it from her. He placed it in the hat and pulled it out so that it went back to normal. "What are you doing here, anyway?"

"I live here, Bostwick, and this happens to be my garden, so—"

"I meant why are you bothering us?"

"I wanted to see what Sebastian has been up to."

"Did he send a letter, too!" Millicent asked. "I completely forgot about the rest of the mail. Let's see…" She rifled through the letters to find his, ripped open the envelope, and glanced over the page, her mouth changing from a smile to a wide gape. She read it over once again, then handed the letter to Bostwick.

"He said the contract is canceled! He didn't say how, though."

"What?" Delilah asked, snatching the letter before Bostwick could read it. "What happened to Chiaroscuro! What happened! Bostwick, transport me there at once!"

"I don't know how to do that," Bostwick muttered, but the queen had already floated up several yards in the air to squint at the horizon over the trees.

"It appears to still be standing," she said, returning to the ground. "Sorry, I thought that something terrible must have happened to it, thus breaking Alcea's promise to protect it."

"Maybe Alcea finally let him go," Millicent said brightly.

"Not likely," Bostwick said. "There must have been some kind of loophole."

"Whatever the reason, Sebastian's free! Delilah, do you think he can come back here soon?"

"Heck no," the queen said, folding her arms. "He's not

allowed back until he grovels at my feet. That's what I told him. Those are the terms of his sentence."

"But you've changed sentences before," Millicent said, tilting her head towards Bostwick.

The queen sighed, took a seat across from them and examined Millicent's hat.

"That's true. I have."

"So he can come back?"

"We have no way of contacting him. Besides, did you read the end of his letter? He said he met up with some Chiaroscurans. They're probably all bonding and having wild adventures. Let's let them be for a while."

She got a far-off look and stared into the sky. Bostwick was about to ask Millicent to try the trick again, when Delilah asked, "Remember when we had that conversation, Millie, before you got kidnapped, about letting Bostwick go after he taught you every trick?"

"I'm surprised you still remember that, Delilah."

"I remember important things. At the time, I agreed to it because I figured that because Bostwick could not do the rabbit trick, he couldn't teach it to you and could therefore never leave."

"Wow," Bostwick said flatly.

"Well, this system obviously is just too complicated, since we now know that there are all sorts of unknown spells out there. I say we go back to Bostwick's annually determined sentence."

"So essentially," Bostwick said, "you're telling us nothing has changed."

"No, I'm clarifying how long you have to stay here. What

with Chiaroscuro coming into Styx, and getting the Empire to look into this new-fangled 'electric lighting', and giving the police a raise, and sorting out that incident with the fishmonger and the mushroom merchant—"

"That was pretty complicated," Millicent added.

"—well, there's hardly been any time to think of my poor neglected butler."

"You bother me ten times a day," Bostwick said.

"Anyway, I've finally had a moment's peace and have totaled up the years of your sentence. Now, it was fifty at last count, yes? Then let's say, oh, down to twenty for your help with Sebastian and Alcea, factoring in workman's compensation. Down to ten for just being Bostwick and making Millie happy every day." He rolled his eyes. "Hmm, you helped fix the clock-window in the throne room, discovered the true identity of the Midnight Stalker last month, and took a pie to the face in place of Millie."

"We all know you were aiming for me anyway."

"Stuff and nonsense, Bostwick. You're a regular hero. So, your total sentence left over is: one year."

"Really?" Millicent asked, beaming. "So next spring, he'll be free?"

"Not *next* spring. Last year at this time was when he became my butler, give or take a month. I honestly can't remember the details. Let's say next week. Yes, next week, it will have been exactly one year ago that you became a thief by stealing my Domino, and it will be next week that the sentence will officially be up."

After this proclamation, she stood up, wandered over to the hedge maze, and became absorbed in the foliage.

"You're serious?" Bostwick asked suspiciously. "You won't suddenly change your mind and add a thousand years to my sentence or use the Domino to turn me into something horrible?"

"Of course I'm serious," she said without turning around. "You'll be absolutely free. You can do whatever you want. You can even go back to Camellia, or the Capital. I know you want to."

Bostwick and Millicent exchanged glances.

"Millie can go, too," Delilah said when she was met with no response, "to the Academy."

"So that's what that letter was about!" Millicent cried. The queen held up a hand and turned around. Her head was down so that her pink bangs obscured her expression.

"I know you told Wilfrock you didn't want to, but we all know it was your feelings for the heretofore imprisoned Bostwick that made you say so."

"No, it's not, Delilah. I love living in Styx."

"Well, Bostwick doesn't. He's always hated it here. And you'd probably like it in Camellia. You could perhaps be co-court magicians, once you graduate."

Bostwick stood up, but Delilah cut him off.

"Don't say anything, Bostwick. You were right about letting Millie go to the Academy, and I was… not as quick at coming to the same correct conclusion. But I have now. Millie wants to go to the Academy, and you want to be with her, and… and I want you both to be happy."

He breathed an annoyed sigh and approached Delilah. Without a word, he reached out and tore the Domino off her face.

She looked at him, her eyes wide with surprise, and said, "Wha—"

He tossed the mask over the side of the hedge maze, and waited two seconds, which was how long it took for Delilah to grab him by the shoulders.

"What did you just do, Bostwick!"

"What are you going to do, curse me?"

"Yes, I'll curse you, you traitorous, thieving—"

She stopped and blinked several times, a look of genuine shock on her face.

"M-Millie?" She turning to Millicent as if to ask her opinion of what had just transpired.

"Just because they let me take the exam again," Millicent said, shrugging, "doesn't mean I won't fail. On purpose, maybe."

The queen bit her lip, at a loss for words, then punched Bostwick in the arm. It hurt immensely, but he could tell it was meant in a friendly way.

"I could curse you, Bostwick. *Should* curse you, in fact. But I'm not going to, yet. No, instead, I think I'll make you work for me for, hmm, two hundred years, with time off for vacation and travel. Why, I'm feeling so generous that I'll even add a salary. Yes. Sounds good. Shall we shake on it, you contemptible thief?"

"That depends, will I be working as a butler, or a magician?"

"If you hadn't thrown my Domino over the hedge, *maybe* you could have been a magician."

"I don't know. I would really prefer—"

"Shake my hand, man!"

He did so, figuring that Delilah would eventually come around. She grasped his hand, then threw her arms around him, hugged him just long enough for him to hear her purring, and then ordered the hedge to move so she could search for the Domino.

Bostwick barely had enough time to straighten his shirt and tie before he heard someone yell, "Congratulations on your new job, Dogsbody!" He turned towards the castle to see Mr. Charles coming towards them. Emmaline followed behind, looking slightly mortified.

"We were listening in on your conversation," Mr. Charles explained cheerily.

"It wasn't my idea!" Emmaline said. "But still, congratulations."

"Emmaline!" Millicent cried, hopping up and hugging her. "When do you get here?"

"A while ago, but Delilah had to chew us out—as representatives of the Empire—for the electric panic incident before we could do anything else."

"How long will you be staying?"

"Only for a week, unfortunately. The empress was excited to hear my plan for diplomacy and has a whole list of countries we need to visit to establish friendly relations and trade and, well, to address the criminal activity of many of the goblin tourists."

"Oh, dear."

"Don't worry. Mr. Charles has a lot of practice dealing with this sort of thing, even if it was only concerning tea before."

"I think I'll be able to handle myself," he said, taking a sip of tea from the cup that he had brought with him from the library.

"How are things going back in Camellia?" Bostwick asked, straining to keep the picnic blanket down, as the wind began to pick up. "Is the new court magician doing all right?"

"She's definitely not as good as you," Emmaline replied, "but I think she'll do well once she gets used to living with a bunch of royalty. She came from a family of circus performers originally, so—Whoa!"

The picnic blanket flipped over and flew away, dumping its contents onto the ground. The wind roared through the garden, and faintly over its howl they heard a continuous buzz. They looked to the sky, searching for the source of the sound, and saw a huge metal balloon with what appeared to be the hull of a ship suspended from it. The noise no doubt came from a number of enormous propellers that were attached around all sides of the balloon; two at the back were spinning too fast to see clearly, while the rest remained unmoving.

"What is that thing?" Emmaline asked, over the dying wind; the propellers were slowly stopping. "It's got to be as big a twenty of your airships, Delilah."

Delilah, who had emerged from the hedge maze wearing the Domino, stared up at the ship as it came to a floating stop above them. It blocked out the sun, and most of its details were obscured by shadow, but they could still see when a large-eared goblin in goggles peeked over the side of the ship and dropped a rope ladder to the ground

"Dad?" Delilah called.

"Delilah!" Bedlam cried as he made his way down the

ladder. "Delilah, we got your message! Blast that Gremlin and his dirty tricks! But never mind that, I've made an even bigger, better airship!"

He leapt to the ground and threw his hand up to indicate his invention.

"Dad, we sent the message about Spleenbeck months ago!"

"Really? But that pigeon only showed up last week."

"Well, it was sent by Dolly," Bostwick muttered. "Anyway, the danger's over, so there's no need to—"

"Danger!" Bedlam cried. "Who said anything about danger? We're here to get Delilah so she can be part of the war."

"War?"

"With Greml, of course. They can't go stealing our technology without expecting retaliation."

"What?" Emmaline said. "You can't declare war on the whole country. Spleenbeck's the one who stole the ship, and I'm fairly sure he's a criminal even in his homeland."

"Oh really?" Bedlam said, removing his goggles. "Then I guess you haven't heard that the Gremlins have been trying to sell their brand-new airships to the other goblin nations. I thought it sounded suspicious, and then when I received that letter…"

"Okay, maybe they did benefit from Spleenbeck's theft, but that's no reason to go to war. Neither Lesse's Moor nor Styx has any sort of military, most of your citizens aren't trained in combat, and whether you want to admit it or not, the Gremlins have superior weapons technology. If you declared war on them, they would bomb both Styx and

Catawampus to dust, and you know it."

"You've really been studying up for this diplomat thing, huh?" Delilah asked.

"She has," Mr. Charles said, taking another a sip of tea.

"Then you must know that we've got to go to war for the principle of the thing," Bedlam said. "Not to mention that they're making a fortune off my idea."

"Although you make a good point," Mr. Charles said. "You couldn't hope to win with only a single airship and no weapons to speak of."

Bedlam opened his mouth to refute this, but shut it and hung his head.

"That's true," he said, kicking away a pebble despondently. "But I really want to go."

"Wait a minute, Dad," Delilah said. "We have a goblin who knows all about making explosives. She's in the laboratory right now!"

"Delilah! You can't be all right with this!" Emmaline said, but the queen had already run back to the castle.

"Well," Mr. Charles said with a wry smile, "this is a nice way to start off our diplomatic mission."

"We have to do something! I'm the one who let Spleenbeck run off with ship in the first place, and if Styx goes to war over it… Well, I became a diplomat to stop this sort of thing, right? Especially if it's tangentially my fault."

"Don't blame yourself," Millicent said. "Goblins like any excuse to go to war."

"True, true," said Bedlam, "Or at least, planning to go to war. We usually aren't organized enough to get to the actual fighting."

"Maybe," Emmaline mumbled, "maybe we can get to Greml before them, Mr. Charles, and head them off. But without our own airship, we'll never make it in time. We need a diversion."

"While you think of one," Bostwick said, "would you mind letting us get back to our magic practice?"

Millicent threw down the pocket watch again, while Bostwick retrieved their top hats and as much of the picnic as was still salvageable. Mr. Charles struck up a conversation with Bedlam on the mechanics involved in air travel. Emmaline merely stared at the two magicians for several minutes, then smiled widely.

"That's it!" she said. "You've got to get married!"

Millicent looked up from her spell. "We have been talking about that. A spring wedding would be easiest for my family to attend, so we thought next spring—"

"It's spring right now! And then you'll need a long honeymoon. The Opal Islands are nice this time of year. I'll even pay for it."

"We're the diversion, huh?" Bostwick said. "I knew goblins were a bad influence."

"It'll prevent a war."

"Yes, but still."

"All right!" Delilah cried, leading Danika and Misha—who still held the rabbit—to the rope ladder. "All aboard. Let's get this war on the road."

"I've always wanted to go to Greml," Danika said, ascending the rope ladder.

"Why am I coming?" Misha asked.

"You have experience advising royalty," Delilah said.

"You can be the Minister of War!"

"U-um, okay." He carefully climbed up the ladder, holding Reginald to his chest.

"You can't go to war now," Emmaline said in calm voice. "Bostwick and Millicent want to get married first."

"We never sai—"

"*Bost*wick! Is this true?" Delilah cried. "Millie! We'll have to get you a stunning gown. What do humans do for a wedding? It doesn't matter, as you'll have to have a goblin ceremony. Bostwick, how good are you at juggling teapots?"

"I am not."

"Lovely! We'll make the preparations immediately, but… Wait. What about the war?"

"I guess you'll have to postpone it," Emmaline said with a shrug.

Delilah pouted her lips in disappointment, then grinned.

"Dad, you're technically a ship's captain, right?"

"Why, I suppose I am!"

"We are not getting married on that thing," Bostwick said, as Delilah started collecting the fallen food back into the picnic basket.

"We'll discuss it all on board." She shoved the basket into Bostwick's hands. "Millie, didn't you get a new pair of goggles at Rare and Priceless the other day? An excellent time to use them, wouldn't you say?"

Millicent smiled, looking at her shoes.

"It would be fun to ride on an airship again. Not to bomb anyone, of course, but…"

Bostwick stared at her for a moment, then sighed in resignation. "I guess we can at least try to change Delilah's mind on the way there. Stop her from assassinating anyone and starting an international incident."

"Good luck with that," the queen said. "Now get your things, Millie. We'll meet you up in the ship."

"They're going to war," Emmaline said in a dazed voice as Millicent hurried to the castle. "We can't stop them. There's going to be a war."

"Looks like it," Mr. Charles said, sipping his tea. "But I wouldn't worry. Like Bedlam said, most goblin wars fizzle out before any damage is done."

Emmaline didn't hear him.

"There are going to be chapters in Ataxian history books citing me as the cause of the Styx-Greml War. Goblin children will—Wait. Wait a minute! Mr. Charles, you can drive a motorcar, right?"

Delilah rolled her eyes, shook her head, and said, "Mine's parked on the other side of the castle, if you want to use it. But you'd better act fast, if you hope of beating us to Greml."

As Emmaline and Mr. Charles raced to the other side of the castle, Bedlam climbed back up the rope ladder followed reluctantly by Bostwick. Delilah floated up beside him.

"So why are you letting Emmaline use the motorcar?" he asked.

"I like a challenge, Bostwick. Besides, she'll never make it in time. Greml is an island."

"I don't even know what to say to that."

"Oh, Bostwick, you don't have to say anything. Butlers are more for decoration than anything else."

The End

For more information about
the Styx Trilogy (including bonus
stories about the characters), as well as other
writing by Rose Corcoran, visit
rosecorcoranwrites.com

Acknowledgements

Thank you to my family and friends, for supporting me and my writing as you always do, and letting me bounce ideas off of you. Thanks especially to my mom, who edited these beasts and dealt with the fact that many scenes were Frankenstein's monsters, sewn together from the corpses of many old drafts.

A special thanks to my big sister, Claire, for doing the covers. They're each lovely on their own, but are especially beautiful as a set.

And finally, thank you to YOU, the reader, for sticking with me till the end! I hope you enjoyed these books, and will continue to follow my writing from here on out. I have all sorts of exciting things planned!

About the Author

Rose Corcoran works as a library specialist at Flagstaff City – Coconino County Public Library and studies library science at the University of Arizona. *Recast Light* is her third novel. She lives in Flagstaff, Arizona and drinks tea (with milk!) morning, noon, and night.

To contact her, write to
rosecorcoranwrites@gmail.com